The Orchid Hunter

(One Man's Quest for Happiness)

by

Rohini Star

Grosvenor House
Publishing Limited

Annette Brooke is hereby identified as author of this
work in accordance with Section 77 of the Copyright, Designs
and Patents Act 1988

The book cover picture is copyright to Paula Mills

This book is published by
Grosvenor House Publishing Ltd
28-30 High Street, Guildford, Surrey, GU1 3HY.
www.grosvenorhousepublishing.co.uk

A CIP record for this book
is available from the British Library

ISBN 978-1-907211-79-9

Dedication

*This book is dedicated to all those souls
who have ever looked up into the stars...
and simply wondered...*

CHAPTER ONE

My name is Christian and I am a botanist. I love flowers and I love trees. But I particularly love flowers. And the flowers that I love in particular are orchids.

Orchids are just the sexiest flowers on earth.

You've never particularly noticed them?

Unbelievable.

You must search the internet right now. Go look in some Readers Digest book or other. Pop down to your nearest garden centre or round next door and ask your neighbour for a picture – and believe me it will be worth it.

How can I describe an orchid?

How does one describe such a thing of great passion? Fragility...? Beauty...?

The scent? The touch? The feel?

Orchids simply excite.

There is a wonderful book which I keep at my base in Kew Gardens, London, called *The English Herbal Guide* published in 1653.

In it is a line which I often quote to people who appear baffled by my obsession with the flower. It says: "Orchids are hot and moist in operation under the dominion of Venus and provoke lust exceedingly."

Wonderful!

And you must have heard or read the well-documented evidence of people going completely nuts about the flower and succumbing to what is commonly termed 'orchid fever'?

Many authorities say the reason behind this madness is that the flower resembles a unique part of the female anatomy and emits the musky scent of a woman. A man becomes obsessed with the quest to possess the flower, engulf the scent. It can drive one to distraction...

What do I say?

I whole-heartedly agree. And I have been fortunate enough to have been on intimate terms with sufficient numbers of the female species to pronounce that women - as with the flowers - come in all shapes and all sizes, in all colours and succulent scents.

In fact, I wouldn't care to put a number to the amount of ladies I have managed to 'de-flower' over the years - but suffice it to say that I am fortunate enough to be a reasonably good-looking member of the male species.

My age is 36, my hair is still abundant, dirty blond and disastrously curly - although I have realised this does hold a certain appeal.

My eyes are sparkling blue and my face weather-beaten, being as that most of my time is spent outdoors.

My physique is strong. I am slim but fairly muscular and 6ft 1ins tall.

Actually you may well have seen me as I present on a couple of gardening shows on the telly.

Christian Trent Barker.

That's my name.

My most popular show is called Gardener's Paradise.

It's on mid-afternoons during the week, and repeated on the Discovery Channel.

It's not bad, actually.

We get reasonable viewing figures as I've been presenting for about five years and have built up quite a bit of a fan base.

Admittedly the average age of my average fan appears to be around 65 and the favourite clothing of my average fan is green plaid acrylic calf-length skirts and buttoned-up-to-the-neckline cream cardies... but nonetheless I console myself with the fact that I do, at least, have fans - and isn't this how the great Mr Titchmarsh started his burgeoning career...?

Anyway, that's not actually the full-time day job which - as I mentioned earlier on - is happily looking after the world's oldest orchid conservatory in that most gloriously abundant of all earthy places: Kew Gardens, London.

You can find me there most mornings, afternoons, evenings and sometimes even during the night - when I'm waiting for a particularly beautiful specimen to burst into bloom.

I'm the one in the green overalls who usually has his canvassed posterior poking up into the air and his nostrils plunged delightfully into the tender petals of a beautiful Phalaenopsis Newberry Spot.

Either that or I will be perched on a polished dew-wet stone inside the conservatory softly caressing the silken leaves of a Cymbidium Sylvan Candy.

If I'm not there, I'll most definitely be outside shovelling horse manure from one spot to another, or pruning a rose; sitting dreamily under one of the marvellous spreading oak trees or planting new seeds and bulbs in the breathtaking rock garden where I can move seamlessly from Asia to Africa to Australia – or maybe I will be simply leaning on the steel balustrade and gazing into the surging water cascading down the rocks into the lilied pond below. Magic.

In the Spring I plant. In the summer I proudly show. In the autumn I prune and in the winter I sort.

That's my work.

It's simple.

It's intoxicating.

It's pleasurable.

It's my life.

Well… sort of…

I do, of course, have another life.

A personal life.

But that's a bit more… shall we say… complicated…?

I live in a small…no… make that *extremely* small bedsit type apartment that my modest wages allow, quite a bit further down the Thames from Kew.

The apartment is decorated in a way I believe interior decorator-types term as 'minimalistic'.

In the main sitting room I have a spongy cream two-seater leather sofa sitting on a polished dark wooden floor which faces French doors made of the same wood. The door leads onto a small decking area which at the moment is brightened up with a neat border of bright red poppies, golden-yellow marigolds and bobbing scarlet begonia.

The deck sits right on the edge of the Thames with only a riverside walkway and a giant grey steel-barred fence to force separation.

One of my favourite times of the day is when I get back from work, prop up my bicycle in the hallway, crack open a bottle of Becks and sit with my feet up on the round glass coffee table watching the paddle steamers, ferrys and cargo boats gracefully swim up and down the river.

In the spring or summer, if you go out onto the decking, you can see down to Vauxhall Bridge and watch the bright red London buses, the black cabs and the non-stop traffic hurtling across morning, noon and night. Further away you can see the circular steel chaos of the London Eye peeping over the city skyline - beautiful when lit up against a dark night sky - and on a quiet morning you can even hear the chimes of Big Ben.

My pride and joy – a giant plasma TV - sits on one cream wall opposite an antique oak chest of drawers donated by Granny Alice. There are two photographs on the chest, one of said granny who died just last year, and the other, a much smaller picture of my old home: the Suryananda Ashram in California.

Mother and father still live out there six months a year but I have not been back since I fled as a teenager. I don't really want to go into the whys and wherefores - suffice it to say that a spiritual retreat may be a wonderful place for those facing a mid-life crisis and searching for the meaning of life but its no place for a growing teenage boy.

Moving swiftly on to my bedroom - this sumptuous space contains a wonderful King-size Italian creation with black grated head-rest (perfect for gripping on to, should the need arise... if you follow my drift...) and cream duvet. I have a battered oak chest of drawers and matching wardrobe both bought from my other home where dearest mama and papa spend the second part of the year - a little pile on the Yorkshire Moors delightfully named Canterboonarry Hall.

The bedroom also boasts a window running from ceiling to floor: again giving a wonderful view of the river.

The kitchen is tiled to within an inch of its life in aluminium, glass and grey. The surfaces are barely touched and still gleam – cooking is not my strong point.

I have a few friends in the city with whom I share the odd glass of lager – usually on a Thursday night when we all try and kick off the weekend early, although I still find it a struggle to keep up with their voluminous intake, having been reared in the ashram on the evils of alcohol.

The rest of what is laughingly called my spare time, I spend with my nose buried in plant encyclopaedias, on the internet hunting down new species of orchid, or lying back in my squelchy, cream leather armchair with the headphones tuned in and turned on to James Blunt or Morrisey or Coldplay.

Everything would, in fact, be perfect and perfectly simply – were that I were also perfectly single.

And that, dear reader, is where my life gets complicated.

For in truth I would probably be truly happy - if I were truly single.

But I am, in fact, neither truly single - nor truly happy.

My heart is wedded – and has been now for nigh on 18 months – to a beautiful, dark-skinned, almond-eyed Italian girl with the most succulent example of dorsal and lateral sepals that I have ever seen on a woman, and that's before I even dare mention her exquisite labellum.

And those beautiful facets of feline femininity are the sole reason for my life being, well, in all honesty – a downright mess.

Sasha is 32 and used to be one of the producers at the independent television company that puts out my show. She lives in London - but on the more affluent north not south bank. She is down-to-earth, funny, intelligent, articulate, sexy…everything that you would ever want in a partner to be precise.

In fact everything would be perfect bliss – but for the fact that she is married.

Happily married, she says - with twin boys.

Except I know that she is not happily married at all.

How can she be when she has been seeing me on a very regular basis for the last 18 months?

Well, again, I say regular – but what I mean is - as regular a basis as the horrendous situation allows because make no mistake, having affairs with married people really isn't all its cracked up to be…

Our romantic life is taken in snatches. A snog here when the husband is working. A full sesh there when he's working away. And the odd weekend when he visits his mother.

She seems to like it this way.

I have to admit that I did at first but now it's driving me insane.

I'm finding that I want to share more than just sex with her – crazy, I know, being a man and all – but its true.

Like the other day when the spectacular Phragmipedium Pearcei finally burst into flower. I whooped with joy, sprang around the lawn like a demented orang-utan, and then picked up the phone to ring Sash… before I remembered it was Saturday.

Saturday means a no phone day. It's a voicemail day. It's a day when there is no getting hold of her for love nor money.

There are a handful of people on this entire globe who would willingly have jumped up and down with me on that day, sharing my joy.

But my wonderfully knowledgeable colleague Ashok was at home with his family and alas un-contactable, my parents were ensconced in the wilderness of the Scottish Highlands, totally un-contactable and my sister, Yoshoda, was...well, as she has always been – probably up some Himalayan mountain or other and permanently un-contactable.

And anyway, I wanted to tell Sasha.

I knew she would love it and, had she not been married or looking after her boys, or washing up - or something equally mundane. I just knew she would have shot down to Kew as quickly as she could – probably armed with her Z1 camera – and whooped with delight with me.

As it was, all I could do was listen to the voicemail: *"Hello, this is Sasha. I'm sorry I can't answer your call at the moment but please leave a message and I'll get back to you as soon as I can."*

It drives me insane because I know damn well that even if I left a message, there would be no reply until Monday morning earliest. And then it would be a quick and dismissive hello, too busy to talk right now, catch you later...

My alcohol-fuelled friends at the Monkey's Gravel wine bar advise me every Thursday night to give her up – usually more and more vocally as the evening wears on. She'll never leave her husband, they nod sagely, warming to their theme. They've seen it all before. It will all end in tears.

And it's not as though I'm without other offers. Women tend to throw themselves in my direction and I've certainly – as I've said above – had my fair share in the past.

Only this time it's different.

Very different.

Its different because, for the first time in my life, I actually want a woman more than she seems to want me. Bizarre. In fact downright unnatural. Very uncomfortable.

But it appears to be the truth.

And its not as though I have nothing to offer...

Apart from my unquestionable sex appeal, great sensitivity, dashing good looks and immaculate home, I also have a little cash stashed away that was given to me by Granny Alice some years before she passed away - and a rather nifty silver MX5 which is my pride and joy.

So, you see my dear reader, I am not without substance - or, as I have pointed out - other offers.

But, most infuriatingly, the one woman in this whole damned world with whom I would be willing to share my modest stock, appears to have other plans on her mind.

I liken the situation to having a bare, grey, back yard while your next door neighbour owns the most sensuous, exotic garden in the whole wide world... and in that garden is the most stunning artichoke purple and red-lipped orchid you have ever set eyes on.

Your neighbour allows you to see their voluptuous smogfest over the fence, and occasionally you can pop in and drink in the scent of the orchid, closing your eyes in rhapsody as you do...

But you can never own the flower, you can never re-plant it in your own garden, and care for it, cherish it, love it and nurture it. And yet all the time, you are achingly aware that the flower would grow so much stronger, be so much happier and burst with passionate scarlet-lipped blossom if it could be re-planted within your own domain.

It remains tantalizingly close but painfully out of reach.

Believe me, being in love with someone who loves you **but...** is the singular most frustrating, painful, heart-breaking emotion ever.

Ashok thinks I've gone crazy.

He doesn't say much – never does – but the second I start to fill him in on my latest instalment of woe, he simply shakes his head from side to side in that wonderful Indian way, listens politely with his hoe in one hand and plant food in the other, and then offers me words of great wisdom such as:

"Christian, my friend, you have to learn to let go."

Or

"Christian, my friend, if it is meant to be, then it will be."

Or,

"Christian, my friend, we are what we are."

And the latest offering, which came last Tuesday as we were both knee deep in horse manure at the back of the palace, and I was sharing my Monday night disaster with Ashok about how Sasha had promised to call the night before and never did...

"Christian, my friend," he said, wiping his hands down the green overalls.... "Everything has a time. A time to come and a time to go. You can't fight time. You can only learn to embrace it."

And I have to say, dear reader, that that is easy for him to say. Ashok, as far as I am aware, has the perfect life.

He married the girl of his dreams – the beautiful Panmeeta – they have three wonderful children who are all perfectly behaved and gloriously polite, he has a comfortable home and a job to which he is wedded.

Therefore I allow him to quietly lecture me on the wrong doings of having an affair from his ivory tower and I listen politely but I know the old man (I say old, but I'm guessing he could be about 50) has never actually lived and loved in the mad, passionate, all-consuming fashion that I am suffering so I care not to take too much notice.

Instead I thank him for his patience, turn back to the job in hand, usually sigh forlornly and spend the rest of the time chewing over my predicament in my head and with a straw in my mouth, try to formulate a plan while misting the leaves of the golden Lycastes Skinneri.

Today is no exception.

Well, today started off being no exception... until I got a telephone call.

And without wishing to sound too melodramatic that call changed the rest of my life forever - as Ashok observed when I mournfully recalled the conversation to him five minutes later.

He shook his head, wiped a smudge of mud off his face and said in a slow and distant manner: "Christian, my friend, you just never know what is around that corner..."

CHAPTER TWO

You see, she left me.

Well, didn't quite leave... because she was never really here.

What I mean is, for three whole months I have to admit that I had been noticing a distinct lack of warmth in her voice.

As I pointed out earlier, she never rang on Monday night and when she did on Tuesday, it was a bombshell.

"It's over Christian. I've had enough."

"What do you mean you've had enough?"

"I can't cope with it any more. The lying. The deceit. The furtive phone calls and nights away. I'm not sleeping because I'm worrying all the time."

"About what?"

"That Steve will find out. That everything's going to come crashing down. You know what. We've talked about it enough times."

"But you've always been the one to say not to worry. Everything will be fine. You're the one who's persuaded me in the past - remember."

I heard a sharp intake of breath down the mobile and glanced over at Ashok who was standing at the top of the manure pile some distance away and waving something in his hand. I turned my back to continue the conversation.

"Sasha?"

"I know, I know, I know. But things change and..."

"What's changed?"

"Everything, nothing... it's just that I've realised I'm not cut out for this any more. Its easy for you, you don't have anyone to lie to..."

"Easy!" I spluttered. "What's so damned easy about going home alone every night? What's so easy about sitting in your bedsit alone every night knowing the person you love – and who, supposedly, loves you – is cuddled up in the arms of another? What's so easy about not being able to ring that person when you want to or always getting the answering machine...?"

"Exactly, exactly," she butted in. "Which is why this has to end. It's no good for either of us – can't you see that Christian? Its not that I want to..."

I heard the tremor in her voice and that made me more angry.

"Then why do it? I can carry on like this. I don't mind." Suddenly, I felt like a drowning man. There was silence now at the other end of the phone.

"Sasha?"

"Look, I have to go. Goodbye Christian. You know I will always love you. Take care. I'll be in touch..."

"Sasha, no... don't put the phone... Sasha."

There was a click and a whir... and she'd gone.

Just like that.

Gone.

I didn't know whether to laugh or to cry. So I did nothing but stare dumbly at the mobile phone lying brick-like in my hand.

Eighteen months of heaven. Gone. Just like that.

I felt numb.

"Are you alright my friend?"

Ashok had crept up on me and made me jump.

I looked at his concerned face, troubled brown eyes under a furrowed brow, and – startled - felt a teardrop prick the back of my left eye.

"She's dumped me."

He lowered his gaze.

"I'm so sorry." "Yes," I quickly wiped the offending tear from my eye and made play of smoothing my hair while he looked down. "So am I."

We stood, the pair of us, studying the dirty brown earth with tufts of yellowing grass peeping through for quite a few moments. Although autumn, I felt the heat of the mid-afternoon sun start to prickle the back of my neck.

"Shall we move into the conservatory and see to the Zygopetalums?"

This was me talking because you see men - most men - find it very difficult to talk about anything remotely emotional. And here we're talking about rejection. Rejection isn't manly. It's not what happens to you when you're a man. You do the rejecting – not the other way round. And this was rejection – big time.

It was these sorts of thoughts that blundered around in my head as we did the short walk from the grassy lawn into the Princess of Wales Conservatory.

Surrounded by the heady scents of Anguloa, Bifrenaria, Cattleya, and the beguiling jewelled colours of Cymbidium and Gongora, I was about to puff up my chest and re-write history by telling Ashok that it was actually I who had done the dumping – not the other way round as I had first said. No. That was momentary confusion. A slight mis-telling of the real story.

But – fortunately – before I began to make a real fool of myself, Ashok turned to me, shook his head, swept a hand through his hair and said slowly: "Christian, my friend, I meant it when I said that you just never know what is around that corner..."

It brought me back down to earth with a bump.

"But what you must always remember..." and with this he fixed me with those massive chocolate eyes. "Is that everything that happens to you is for your own good. It may not seem it at the time. Indeed what happens to you may cause you a great deal of pain and anguish..."

I dropped my head and stared at the growing hole at the end of my left trainer.

"But you know deep down that the only way you will learn in this life is to live through that pain, learn the lessons that life is teaching you, and move on to greater things, to your highest potential."

I wiped another unwelcome tear away from the corner of my eye. Ashok appeared not to notice.

"If you and Sasha aren't meant to be together," he continued. "Then no amount of pushing or wishing or manipulating will bring you together. But if you are, then it will happen in its own time. Everything has a time and there is a right time for everything. Everything has a reason. There is a reason this has happened. There is a reason for everything. Now is not the right time and for that there is a reason."

His hand reached out and squeezed my upper arm. "Patience, my friend. The reason always becomes clear with time and patience. The old ways always have to clear to make way for the new. Take your time, exercise patience and allow events to unfold. Everything will work out in the right time for the right reasons. Just relax and take your time...There is no need to worry...You'll see..."

CHAPTER THREE

Which was all well and good but realistically how does a young, handsome, semi-famous, virile man bottled with rage, hurt and humiliation, cope with such cold-hearted rejection?

I suppose I could have taken the advice of both Ashok and my parents which was simply to accept my fate in a gentlemanly manner, close the door on sensory distractions, burn some incense sticks, put on some chants and meditate on how everything was planned for my higher good.

Or I could do what I actually chose to – and that was deal with rejection in the time-honoured male way.

I decided to go out every single night of the week, got rip-roaring drunk and bedded every single/married/ white/black/brown/yellow/cherry pink with blue dots on wench in the age range of 18 to 38 in the whole of the capital that I could lay my filthy hands on.

You've heard of the Lost Weekend, well, I had a lost six and a half months.

Pop psychologists would have had a field day.

I lost love so I decided to de-sensitise myself from that over-hyped emotion and fell head-first into a hedonistic whirlpool of sex, alcohol, parties and frenzied colour.

Which was all marvellous to start off with.

The number of friends I could boast on FaceBook went from a lacklustre 73 to a whopping 452 – in the space of two months.

I became the toast – at least in my own head – of the whole damned city.

I had emails, texts and phone calls by the sackload.

However I do have to - slightly shame-facedly - admit that some of the correspondence from my female brethren was of the, perhaps, rather aggressive type.

"You bastard," one said simply.

"Fuck you," was another little epitaph.

"Sod off," a third.

You get the general idea.

But 'love 'em and leave 'em' – that was my new motto. Do as thy would be done by or had been done by. If I could love as strongly as I had done, and still be hurt, then I felt it my duty to let the rest of the female species understand what it felt like.

I was on a mission.

And, of course, it couldn't last.

My belly practically tripled in size with the infusion of lager upon lager upon lager. The bags under my eyes – normally attractive by their parcity – grew into ugly, dark, lined smudges. And I began to get up later and later each day to drag myself into work, an environment where I normally felt so at peace and work which I had so enjoyed, all of a sudden seemed empty and void.

I was a loser and I was getting lost.

I tried to get Sasha back of course during those dark winter months, left voicemails, emails, snail mails. Became a stalker for a short time hiding beneath lamp-posts near her home, desperate just to snatch some sight of her.

Pathetic.

But I couldn't see it.

"Forgive her," Ashok said to me during one of my particularly dark moments. We were hoeing some land in preparation for seeds. I turned to him, feeling my brow furrow. "Forgive?"

"Yes, my friend," Ashok kept his head down and churned up the brown soil in front of him with the hoe. "You must learn to forgive, my friend, and learn to keep loving no matter what harm is done to you."

I kept quiet but felt the anger boil inside of me.

"Don't hold anger and bitterness towards anyone that hurts you as it will only cause you suffering in the end, that is the law of karma – you simply get what you give out. As you sow, so shall you reap."

I looked down at the hoe in my hand, and hung my head.

"You do not want to listen my friend, that is under-standable. But you are in darkness right now and dark-ness is a vacuum, it sucks the life out of itself and everything around it. You need light, light in your heart and in your life. To regain it, you must learn to forgive. Don't forget. Learn your lesson, whatever that may be. But keep the light in your life and learn to forgive, my friend, forgive."

And with that he turned, smiled, and carried on with his hoe. Conversation obviously at an end…

As was usual, the TV work had dried up over the winter months which was unfortunate in one way because I would have gotten to see Sash through work but fortunate on the other hand because I wasn't sure I could summon the energy to bounce around in telly land for more than five minutes.

My lack of interest, enthusiasm or any kind of drive during that half-year episode, did not go unnoticed either.

Ashok, in his wonderful, quiet way, continued to try to offer advice and distraction but I began to become too impatient for his kindly words. It really does embarrass me now to think of the way that I treated him.

But it wasn't just Ashok who noticed the change in my behaviour. It was late on a Friday afternoon at the back end of March that I was summoned to the boss's office.

Colin is a big man brought up in the sixties and seventies by an unenlightened mother on a diet of pizza, baked beans, coca cola and white bread. In the natural way of things he then married a woman equal to the size of his dear mama, and with exactly the same attitude to the fuel of life and its subsequent digestion ie copious quantities digested at the speed and frequency of a rhinoceros in heat.

His admiration for all things edible eventually spewed into his vocational life, and if there was ever a man made for a job, it was he - a world expert on fungi.

Mushroom Man is the nickname handed down by various of his employees over millennium of years, and he fitted the bill well.

I suppose he must have once sported some hair on his head but now the vast majority of it had slipped down to his chin, shoulders and back transforming on its way from a wiry brown mushy colour to a definite turgid grey.

The pinky-brown of his balding head is speckled with darker brown liver spots of varying shapes and sizes – blessing his whole appearance to bear an uncanny resemblance to the Buna Shimeji mushroom. Either that or a sepia globe.

His watery grey eyes are hidden behind beer-bottom glasses held together at either side by two-year-old dirt-encrusted sellotape wound round to the thickness of a double buckle.

Always dressed in a thread-worn forest green cardigan with dark brown baggy trousers and a yellowing checked shirt, he gives the impression of a yokel-local – aided and abetted by a thick Gloucestershire accent.

But, if you ever do get the chance to meet him, do not be fooled.

This man can boast a cutting intellect and a brain so sharp, it almost sears itself in two.

And believe me, what he doesn't know about mushrooms is not worth knowing. The proudest moment of his life was discovering the *Gigantus Florenti Haemorrhoidarius* hidden half way up some tree bark in the mid-1970's. The story of how he and the infamous William Tridon (editor of the now defunct Fungi and Flora magazine) went walking in the New Forest, lost their way and then magically saw the brown and cream sprouting mushroom just before he was stung by a wasp, is legendary – mostly because he tells everyone with the polite patience to listen at every given opportunity.

Having said that, Colin doesn't talk much at all, often preferring to remain glued to the miscroscope and closeted in his rambling, cluttered office at the back of the palace.

Which is why, when you get a call from him, you take notice. He is not one to waste his breath on words.

When I appeared in his office that late March afternoon, I found him in his natural position, hunched up over the microscope, cardigan buttons askew and mouth open dripping spots of saliva onto the stained wooden desk.

"Come in," he bawled, long after I had entered.

"Siddown," he motioned to a sunken armchair in one corner of the office, its former orange glory torn to a scruffy heap by one of his two massive black Labradors which frequented the office with their owner but were now both curled in front of the three-bar electric fire in the corner.

I moved some offending dog hairs from the chair, surreptitiously curled up my nose at the offending acrid smell of cigarette smoke, dog and damp mixed with an unhealthy smattering of BO - and sat, waiting.

Eventually – and after much huffing and puffing - he managed to tear his gaze away from the microscope, straightened his back with one arm bent behind him to support the manoeuvre, and ambled round to the front of his desk where he surveyed me through screwed-up eyes.

"I've noticed," he said at length. "That you have not been quite yourself recently."

I did nothing but hang my head slightly – I couldn't argue.

"Now then," he continued, pushing the broken glasses back up his nose with a dirty finger which boasted a yellow fingernail stained from years of smoking 20 a day Benson and Hedges. "I've been wondering what to do about this unfortunate set of circumstances."

"Oh?" I started - bemusement that he had noticed anything beyond the boundaries of a petra dish evaporated into shock that he intended to take action against any offending state I was in.

Colin screwed up his eyes to an even tighter degree and peered at me hard.

"I mean," he drawled. "That we can't let the situation continue."

"I...I...I..." I could hear myself doing an embarrassing rendition of a blubbering three-year-old and noticed, as though from a distance, that my hands had tightened their grip on the arms of the chair.

Colin put up his flabby hand to stop me going any further.

"Stop your panicking," he protested. "I'm not talking about sacking you."

I felt a rush of relief to my shoulders which must have visibly dropped from around my ears. Despite messing around for the last six months fighting a nervous breakdown and being blasé about my work (to say the very least), I did still love my job and didn't want to lose it.

"No," he continued, turning to pick up various sheets of A4 paper which lay scattered across his desk. "No, fortunately for you, you're far too good to be let go of but we need to do something... and I was wondering how you liked the Amazon?"

"The Amazon?"

"Yes – the jungle?"

"The Amazonian jungle?" I gaped back at this lump of a man barely able to comprehend his words.

Colin shuffled over to my armchair and thrust the papers in my hand.

"Go away and think about it," he instructed to my open-mouthed façade. "Read these papers, its all in there. I think you need a new challenge, a shot in the arm to get your interest back in the job. We think you could find the Dendrophylax Lindenii."

I felt my mouth drop wider.

"It's a very rare orchid."

"I know what it is," I stuttered, finally gathering my senses. "The Ghost Orchid... its beautiful... but..." I felt my brows knit. "It's in Florida."

Colin paused, peered at me hard, and walked back to his desk.

"Not any more it isn't. There have been sightings in South America of what could be a new strain and we need Kew to have the find. I want you and Ashok to go to the Amazon basin, and bring back a cutting. If you're interested, you will leave in two days time. The air tickets are booked. I was going to go myself but..." his voice trailed away and he looked down at the floor.

"I can't believe this," I gasped. "You're asking me if I want to go to the Amazon, to search for a Ghost Orchid and bring it back to Kew?"

Colin frowned. "I thought they told me you were bright."

"I'm sorry," I stumbled, struggling out of the chair. "It's just that... I can't believe... I mean."

"Look lad," Colin had ambled back to the other side of the desk and was preparing to hunch up again behind the microscope. "Go away and think about it. I don't need an answer right away. Talk to your family. Talk to your wife or partner, kids – I don't know. But let me know first thing tomorrow."

"And Ashok?" I said, grabbing hold of the door handle. "What has he said?"

"His family has said its fine, he's just waiting to see whether you want to go." And with that Colin glued his left spectacle to the microscope which I took as my sign to leave.

"Fine, great, thank you. Right. I'll let you know," I swung open the door and banged it shut, leaping down the back stairs two at a time. Reaching the bottom I punched the air and then felt that habitual stirring in my stomach. I had to phone Sasha.

Hands shaking, I pulled out my mobile and dialled the number. This just wasn't an excuse, no, I reasoned. This was a sort of emergency. She would be cross if I had just disappeared off into the tropical back-of-beyond without even a by-your-leave.

The phone rang for an eternity. Then finally:

"Hello."

Silence on the other end.

"Hello," I say again, louder.

"Christian...?... Is that you?"

Thank God. At least she still recognised my voice.

"Yes, hi... how are you?"

"I'm well, thank you... you?"

Hoorah, she was wanting to engage in conversation. This was better than I had hoped.

"Good, good," I said, feeling my shoulders relax back into their natural place – away from my ears. "You?"

"Not bad, its nice to hear from you."

Nice? *Nice?* What sort of a mediocre word is nice? I would have much preferred 'wonderful' 'fantastic' or even the more mundane 'lovely' but... *nice*????

"Well, I just thought... you know..."

Suddenly I felt stuck for words. I knew what I wanted to ask her – well, tell her really... that I was going away into the jungle searching for a rare and beautiful orchid, and that the trip was jam-packed with unimaginable danger so she would have to beg me to stay.

What I said was: "I'm going away."

"Oh? That's nice."

There - that awful, innane word again. It should be banned from the dictionary.

"Yes."

"Anywhere interesting?"

"The Amazon."

"Gosh."

At last I had her attention.

"Well... be careful..."

She was concerned. I could hear it. I was ecstatic.

"I'll try."

"You ok?"

My head somersaulted. She was interested in my well-being. I knew it. I knew the whole break thing had been a mistake. I knew that deep down she still loved me. I knew we just had to be together somehow. Someday...

"Not bad," I tried to keep my voice sounding cool but knew there was a distinct tremor and had to clear my throat. "You?"

"I'm alright."

She sounded anything but...

"Listen Christian, I'm awfully sorry but I'm going to have to disappear, we've just had a short break but I'm going to have to pull the team together otherwise we'll never get this shoot finished."

"Ok, right."

I felt a lump in my throat.

"I'll go then."

"Yes, fine, ok," I think. I'm sure I heard. I'm almost sure there was a distinct tremble in her voice. "Have a good trip...."

And that was it, the click and brrrr of the phone, and she was gone.... Again.

I turned to see Ashok silhouetted in the doorway of the building.

"We go, my friend?" he said simply.

I bowed my head and clenched a fist.

"Yes Ashok," I replied. "We go."

CHAPTER FOUR

The night before we left, I did a strange thing.

I was at Canterboonarry Hall and was busy packing when I went up in the attic to find some old binoculars that my father used to use for his ornithological interests.

Instead I found my old diaries. Diaries and letters.

Ones I had kept during mine and Sasha's affair.

They read like a cross between a Mills & Boon, and a dirty Black Stocking number.

Take for instance, this letter that I sent to Sasha one year into our affair – she'd just left Gardener's Paradise and got a new job producing Nature's Nooks and Crannies. All her energy was being poured into her work and I was finding it very difficult...

Hello Sasha,

I have so much to say that I don't know where to begin.

For the past few days I have been thinking a lot about our time spent together.

I was remembering – as I told you - walking down the Euston Road together in London and me pulling you over to look at all the hi-fi shops.

I was remembering – as I told you – taking you to Edinburgh for your birthday last year and getting up to all sorts in the hotel before going on the shoot.

And then I started to remember other things too.

I remembered walking hand-in-hand through Whitby after you'd tried to break my fingers at the little tapas bar and we'd laughed out loud alongside the waiters.

I remembered thinking how much I still fancied you as we toured around an old gun battery, in the sunshine earlier in the day.

I remembered meeting up with you on the South Bank on a Sunday after I came back from holiday and being so happy to see each other.

I remembered being in the car on the way to Liverpool once and you saying that you wanted to tell me so much but held back all the time and me desperately wanting to know what it was you wanted to say…

I remembered all the naughty, silly phone calls late at night that used to go on for hours whenever you were working and driving home a long way round so we could carry on talking.

The letter carried on but I couldn't read any more so I swept up some more papers from out of the diary box, stuffed them in my bag to read later, and headed back downstairs.

CHAPTER FIVE

We set off for South America at four o'clock the following day. Me, Ashok and, what appeared to be a full shed-load of baggage. Mostly mine it has to be said but then I never believed in the old adage of travelling light. Ridiculous idea.

After all, one has 'things' and these 'things' need to be taken with one to remind one of one's own importance… don't you think?

Ashok certainly didn't think so.

His baggage consisted of one simple, black, shoulderbag which only appeared half-full.

"Do you really require all those suitcases, my friend?" He looked at the bags with a perplexed frown on his face as we stood in the queue waiting to be checked in.

I glanced down to where my four tattered brown suitcases stood shoulder to shoulder on the floor next to us.

"Yes," I replied defensively. "They have been right around the world with me on many occasion and they will continue to do so today… There are things in there that I need." I added for extra surety.

Ashok shrugged and said nothing.

After a full 50 minutes wait, we finally got to the front of the check-in and I spent another 20 minutes arguing with the airport person about the amount he was charging for my extra baggage. Outrageous.

Ashok waited patiently for me to finish and then we walked into the departure lounge.

"Excess baggage always holds us up and makes us pay out more – in airports and in life," he said cryptically before winking and walking away to the Gents.

CHAPTER SIX

I won't bore you too much dear reader with the whys and wherefores of our arrival in Bolivia, suffice it to say that the jungle was everything you would imagine – hot, green, lush, hot and hot.

And our journey there was horrifically long, turgid, bumpy and terrifying.

The tiny airstrip where we landed frightened me to death as did the even smaller aeroplane that transported us into the thick of the jungle.

We spent one extremely uncomfortable night in a ramshackle hut decorated with giant lizards, spiders and indescribable amphibious mammal things (the names and nuances of God's wonderful moving critters have never been my strong point - give me a green-leafed stable, above-all silent creation any time instead).

Then the following morning one of the guides handed us a torn, yellowing stiff piece of paper which disguised itself as a map, and pointed a scrawny finger in the direction of a tiny break in the green foliage – allegedly a path.

And that was it.

We were on our own.

In the middle of the Amazon.

At the start of an adventure...

We had enough supplies to last us for about 10 days - although we reckoned we should be somewhere in the region of the Ghost Orchid after about four or five days of walking.

"Isn't one of the guides coming with us?" I asked of Ashok as I watched the two native South American's move away back to the hut.

"We don't need a guide, my friend," came the short reply.

"Why? Have you been here before?"

I swung my faded green ruck-sack on my back (having finally heeded my good Indian friend's advice about excess baggage, the four large brown bags were now safely housed back in the hut near the airfield), turned to face my travelling companion and felt a grin spread across my face.

"No," he smiled back. "But we have a map and we have our hearts and souls to guide us. We do not need anything more."

I shook my head – partly in disbelief and partly in admiration. "Well, I suppose the orchid shouldn't be that deep in the jungle and we do have plenty of food."

"We will be fine, my friend, don't worry, everything will be just as it is meant to be."

I felt the grin creep back on to my face. "I guess you're right mister philosophical. I guess you're right... and I guess this is where our journey begins."

The heat and stomach-clenching terror of the plane ride here was already starting to recede and the knot in my stomach was now one of excitement rather than panic-stricken anxiety.

Ashok looked up from where he had bent down to tie his bootlace and grinned back.

"The journey never stopped my friend. It has no beginning and no end. Never concentrate on the destination, just enjoy the ride...."

"I know, I know, I know," I interrupted, feeling my good mood dissolve. "But this is a different part of the journey. Ah-ha – in fact each day is a new beginning!" I felt pleased with my cleverness in twisting around Ashok's words... but not for long.

I waited for the response but my Indian companion simply smiled, straightened his back, slung on his own rucksack and walked right past me towards the path.

"What?" I said, disappointed at his silence. "No words of wisdom? No retort? Nothing?"

Ashok stopped and turned to face me, a smile breaking across his face.

"We both have a long way to go on our journeys," he said. "But one thing I do know is that while I can share some points of wisdom with you that I myself have managed to pick up on the way, I cannot tread your path – you must do that yourself. If some things make more sense to you than others, then obviously those words are meant for you and will resonate with you. Do not follow in others footsteps. Think your own thoughts, my friend, feel your own feelings, beat your own drum... that is the way to consciousness and a new awakening."

And with that, he turned back to the path and set off at quite an amazing rate for a man of his age.

I pondered his words for a few seconds but they didn't weigh me down, they made me feel lighter, and as I took my first proper steps into the jungle, I felt the sun on my face and excitement in my belly.

CHAPTER SEVEN

Disappointingly the good feeling didn't last.

After four sweltering days and three sleepless nights, I was beginning to feel the pain, and desperately wishing I was curled up again under my king size cream duvet in my Thames-adjacent home.

Ashok, on the other hand, never ceased to amaze me.

He slept like a baby every night, woke up seemingly refreshed every morning and bounced along the footpaths with the light step and swing of a man more than half his age.

I was genuinely impressed and wanted to know his secret.

"Diet." He replied simply when I finally got around to questioning him as we fought our way through palm leaf fonds later that day.

"Diet?" I repeated, feeling puzzled.

"Yes. Vegetarian."

"And that's what gives you all this energy?"

"Good food, good digestion, good thoughts, good deeds, good energy."

I pondered on his words as I swept a disturbingly large black spider off my fore-arm and ducked as a strand of green foliage nearly took off my left eyebrow. "Sounds a bit dry..."

Ashok laughed – he did that a lot.

"Depends on your attitude," he replied, then stopped and turned to look at me with his eyes partly closed. "Everything depends on your attitude, my friend."

He turned back and we carried on walking in silence for a mile or so as I chewed over his words. I had come to realise that Ashok said barely anything in jest; that everything did - in fact - mean something, and that I would be wise to listen properly and fully understand before I tackled him on any other subject.

Everything depends on your attitude obviously meant adopting a positive attitude to all situations no matter how testing. But I still wanted to know how that actually manifested itself into such physical fitness.

"Ashok?"

"Yes"

"Do you mind if we take a break?"

We walked a few paces further to a natural clearing in the forest floor. I sat down with my back against the red bark of an enormous tree, and took a swig from the water bottle which we judiciously refreshed every time we came across a stream or river or watering hole.

Ashok, as was his usual manner, simply sat very still and very upright in a cross-legged position with his eyes closed and a semi-smile playing across his lips.

"What do you mean by good digestion?" I asked after a few minutes.

The half smile broke into a huge grin.

"Eat at regular times, sitting down and concentrate on each mouthful. Chew your food fully before swallowing and give thanks for each morsel. Eat a large meal when the sun is highest in the sky, use the fire of the sun to heat the fire of your digestive juices, then eat little as the day wears on. Rise at six with the sun and sleep at sundown. Drink warmed water, never take ice in your drinks as that cools and blocks the system. That's good digestion."

I pondered his words.

"It's not always possible to have the biggest meal of the day in the middle of the day," I ventured, trying hard not to sound too negative.

"Nothing is impossible," came the swift retort.

True, I acknowledged silently in my head.

"So what about the thoughts, deeds and energy?"

There was another long silence before finally Ashok closed his eyes fully and said: "You must always watch your thoughts because your thoughts become your reality. Good thoughts produce good deeds, good energy and a positive reality. The reverse is true of negative thoughts."

A frog croaked by my feet, startling me.

"Good thoughts, deeds and energy will lighten your load and lighten your heart eventually leading to physical fitness. You cannot have a light mind and a heavy body, the two must equate."

"Right," I said slowly.

"Your body really is your temple my friend," Ashok opened his eyes and stared intently at me. "You must remain healthy in body to be healthy in mind. Let not laziness or depression drag you down. Always resolve to meditate, to pray, to be grateful for all of your blessings, to be thankful for everything that you eat and everything that you have – and make sure that food is full of energy itself and not processed to death. Finally, enjoy and be thankful for every single second of your day, for every breath you breathe.

"This life is for living, to waste it on negativity is a sin. See joy in everything you do, feel joy in everything you are. Live in the moment and for the moment... for what else is there?"

And with that, he shut his eyes once more indicating that particular conversation was closed.

CHAPTER EIGHT

Closed – but not forgotten.

I spent many a day following that conversation thinking about what he had said as we trekked deeper and deeper into the jungle.

I thought a lot about the way in which I had lived my life back in London. I had actually spent nearly all the time since I broke up with Sasha literally abusing my body. I was drinking way too much alcohol and living off processed, packaged food which hadn't seen natural sunlight for weeks never mind days.

I had also stopped biking into work and always caught a bus. I had spent the days moaning or getting angry and the nights getting wasted so I didn't have to think.

Deep in the jungle with not a single distraction and only one focus, I suddenly had clarity about the way in which I was literally destroying a life I should be celebrating – and it was quite a wake-up call.

"Do you really have to be vegetarian?" I said to Ashok one evening over a meal of dry bread, bananas and water.

Ashok paused to finish what he was eating before replying. "The human species is not actually built to eat meat - if you look at the way in which our teeth are designed compared to other carnivores, there is no correlation.

"You also need to think of everything in an energetic way. By digesting meat you are taking in the energy of the animal that has been killed – probably not in a natural way - and all the fear from that animal at its time of death is transmuted into its every cell, its blood, its brain, its muscle... therefore its meat. Eating that animal, you digest that meat and that energy."

"But can't you say the same of plants?" I taunted.

Ashok paused again before answering. "You could," he agreed. "Although plants are not of such a high consciousness as an animal so there is not so much of the negative energy. My best advice to you – as always – is to follow your own heart, listen to your own body. Don't be swayed by following the crowd or fashion, seek your own clarity."

I thought about that for a second...

"But you don't always know what you want."

"Then you must quieten down all the hustle and bustle in your life to hear because your heart does always know the best way, the quickest route, the right thing to do. Don't dull your senses with alcohol, with drugs, with processed food, loud music and constant inane chatter and gossip. Quieten the mind and you will hear your heart speaking to you, guiding you, letting you know what you must do and how to do it.

"Your heart will guide your soul, your spirit and your body to a higher place, and to peace."

I nodded, taking it all in – I knew I was certainly becoming clearer about things in my own head as my time in the jungle wore on so now what I needed to do was to decide what it was I actually wanted.

Ashok appeared to read my thoughts.

"Once you have managed to calm down your mind by switching off the television and the computer, by staying indoors instead of going out, by drinking pure water and juices instead of the alcohol, then you can start to meditate more and go quiet, to ask questions which will be answered, to look for signs and guidance and to trust your intuition which is your heart showing you your path.

"Watch those signs, listen to those feelings, and write down what it is you feel is important to you. Make a list or cut out pictures in magazines and stick them on to a board then every morning read the list or look at the board and you will be reminded of your goals, you will stay focussed, and you will use every second and minute on this earth wisely and accomplish many things."

I took a large bite of my bread and nodded thoughtfully as I allowed his words to sink in.

CHAPTER NINE

The days wore on with any conversation at all growing more and more sparse, and the hot, humid density of the jungle growing thicker and thicker.

I was beginning to lose track of time and I'm not sure exactly when it was that it began to dawn on me that we could be lost.

Hopelessly lost.

Lost in the sense that every single branch, tree, flower and fauna started to look exactly the same as the last.

Lost in the sense that the compass had become plain annoying rather than an instrument of any use.

Lost in the realisation that panic had not yet started to grab hold but was certainly hovering vulture-like on the distant horizon.

Lying on my bed one evening, I gazed up at the dense foliage above and tried to force down the gnawing sense of unease that was beginning to seep into my stomach walls.

"I miss the stars," I said, almost by way of making conversation and quelling the rising angst.

There was silence, broken only by the jungle sounds of tree frogs squawking and far-away monkeys chattering.

My stomach started to rumble and, in a bid for distraction, I carried on with attempting a conversation.

"Do you ever watch the stars at night Ashok?"

Another pause before the man who I had travelled with for the last 10 days, who I had worked with in close proximity for the previous four years, who I thought I knew almost as well as I knew myself, rolled over, turned to me and said: "Watch the stars Christian? Do I watch the stars? I have watched the stars since I was so small that I fitted into my mother's glove. I have watched the stars since I first opened my eyes. I have never stopped watching the stars. I am an astrologer."

His answer astounded me and I sat up and leant on my elbow studying the outline of his face in the gloom with a sense of awe and amazement.

"Western?"

"Vedic."

"Jyotish?"

Now it was Ashok's turn to be surprised.

"You know Jyotish?"

I leaned back on my pillow, put my hands behind my head and stared into the growing darkness under the canopy of trees.

"Ashok, I was brought up in an Ashram. My father was a Vedic Astrologer. I am Scorpio rising with Moon and Sun in Leo. I grew up with Indian Astrology - Jyotish."

The only sound that could be heard was the swish of a monkey's tail as it leapt in the tree canopy above us, probably bending the branches and clinging on for dear life.

"That is truly remarkable my dear friend. Forgive me, but there are not many Western people who know of Jyotish."

I quietly reflected on his remark.

"I have never spoken about it with anyone."

"Nor are you likely to. Jyotish is the most important tool in human learning known to mankind and yet it is too complex for many to consume. It allows us to see and shape our destinies, to connect with universal forces and to become acutely aware of our place in the universe. To know of Jyotish is the highest privilege, to help others with that knowledge is more so.

"My only regret is that in these days it is either unknown in the West or it is belittled and scorned. In the East it is often viewed as little more than an oracle for decision-making on trivia. Only the wise, the elderly and sincere truth-seekers are open to its deepest teachings... and that troubles me."

A parrot screeched in the distance and we both fell silent.

It was Ashok who spoke again first.

"Where is your father now?"

"Here and there."

"He left you?"

I sighed. This night was going to be a long one.

"I left him. Him, my mother and my sister."

"Oh."

"I was 16, Ashok, and I had had enough." I tried to explain my actions of two decades ago but still felt weighed down by the effort. "I had had enough of the spiritual life, of the searching for meaning, of the peace and serenity, the yoga, the meditation, the goodness of it all..."

"It's what most people spend their lives searching for."

"I know." I still felt guilty after all these years about turning my back on most people's idea of paradise.

"But it was not your karma to be there."

I looked at him in amazement for the second time that evening and sat up sharply.

"Exactly," I said excitedly. "That is what I tried to say. That is how I felt. Everybody has karma. Everyone has a purpose and mine was to be out there, to live life, to be a normal teenage boy."

"Ahhh." Ashok held up his finger which silenced me. "You must know from all your teachings though that that bit is not true."

I hung my head.

"A life purpose is not selfish. It is to serve others for the higher good. Therefore I expect you were not meant to live in the Ashram but you were meant to stay there long enough to be able to soak up the message and then come out into the Western world maybe to spread that message...?"

"I don't know... if that's the case, I haven't made a very good job of it have I?"

Ashok paused and studied his hand. "You are young," he said finally. "There maybe all sorts planned for you of which you are not fully aware."

We both fell silent again.

After a few minutes Ashok spoke. "So, your father was an astrologer?"

"Yes,"

"So he would have been able to foresee your running away."

I considered the question. "He said that he had seen it in my chart but..."

"He lived in an Ashram for six months of the year and studied as a Vedic Astrologer. He WOULD have foreseen your future."

I was a little taken aback at the ferocity of Ashok's words.

"I guess," I mumbled.

"And he accepted that future because there is no other way than acceptance and he could probably see what was to come later in life."

I hung my head. "That is what he said," I concurred.

In the growing darkness I could just make out Ashok fingering a long blade of grass, seemingly deep in thought.

"So although you ran away, you never totally lost touch."

"No. I still see my parents fairly frequently at their house in Yorkshire."

"Ah."

He had fallen quiet again and I was getting impatient.

"Ashok, what is it that you are getting at? What are you trying to say?"

"I'm sorry. I'm not trying to be secretive. I was simply trying to work out your chart and what your father saw for you, your life journey to this point and your soul purpose."

"No wonder you were quiet!" I tried to jest but my light-hearted attempts fell on deaf ears.

"Where are the other planets in your chart?"

I was used to these questions and – despite my outward indifference – did know my horoscope back to front.

"Mars in the 12th…"

"Libra."

"Jupiter in the 8th, Saturn in the 4th, Venus in the 11th and Rahu/Ketu axis 1st and 7th. Finally Mercury goes into the 9th."

"Dharma karma yoga," muttered Ashok under his breath. "Your dasha?"

"Mars dasha but going into Rahu anytime now."

Ashok looked at me and narrowed his eyes. "Did your father explain about dashas and transits, he must have done."

I nodded. "A long time ago."

"Dashas and transits map out the timeline of your life in the chart. Rahu is in your seventh house of relationships, tenth from the tenth which is your house of career where sits the Sun, your soul and the place where you shine, and Moon, your emotional and spiritual self in the fire sign of Leo. Rahu is all about going to excess – in your case in relationships but linked with your career. You are about to enter a Rahu dasha – which focuses the energy of that planet - at the same time as the bountiful Jupiter enters your seventh house."

I could feel Ashok staring at me through the darkness with extreme intensity. I lowered my eyes.

"I feel my friend," he said finally. "That this little adventure is only the start of a much bigger adventure for you. Now let us get some sleep."

Chapter Ten

Easier said than done.

My dreams that night were in turmoil.

There was a bulldozer high above my head with its black jaws wide open ready to crash down and gobble me up. There were a line of carrion crows, beaks sharpened on a wall. And there was a spider crawling along the ceiling. I dreamed of swirling planets, dazzling Suns, shooting stars and dark, black holes.

I woke earlier than usual - sweating and totally disorientated. For a minute I thought I was back in my London flat, having fallen asleep on the sofa but glancing around in the early morning mist, I came to my senses and felt my heart sink.

We were still in the jungle, still lost, still not knowing whether we would ever be found.

Not only that but if my calculations were correct, it was Sasha's birthday today.

This time last year we had celebrated – not on the day itself of course, that was left for the children and *him*. No. We had celebrated two days later by going back to my little apartment, drinking a half-bottle of pinot plonk and having what can only be described as the best sex EVER for nigh on three hours... before she had to leave.

"Its so unfair," I had moaned, standing in the doorway of the bathroom watching her glide her black stockings on one after the other whilst leaning seductively over the sink.

"Life's unfair," she had answered, smiling mischievously through black fronds of ruffled hair.

I had lifted my hand to smooth down her hair and found my fingers running down the nape of her neck.

The mischievous smile had turned to a frown.

"Not now Christian. I have to go."

I felt my heart sink at the rebuke, even though I was no stranger to the situation.

"I'll call you."

She had pulled her skirt up, quickly flung on her black overcoat and was out of the door in a flash.

The door banged shut hard and there I was again – left alone.

Struggling to free myself from the despair of my memories, I glanced over to a waterfall just upstream from where we had made camp and saw Ashok already sitting on a rock in his customary lotus position, deep in meditation. He looked immensely peaceful and I felt a strong pull to join him.

Stretching out, I threw off the thick brown blanket, pulled on my boots and jacket – the morning still held a chill – and walked to Ashok's side.

"Sit down my friend," he murmured as I reached the rock. "It would be good for you to be still. Do you want me to guide you?"

"There is no need," I replied. "I am not quite ready."

Ashok smiled although his eyes were still closed.

"I know," he said simply.

So I sat cross-legged on a rock in front of a waterfall in the middle of the Bolivian jungle with an Indian man on the birthday of my former lover ... and I wept silently as he meditated.

CHAPTER ELEVEN

The following day it began to rain. Not just a little rain but torrential, drenching, downpouring rain. Rain that not only soaked your skin but your very bones. Fortunately we had managed to get up and dressed before it started – wakened by the calls of many strange animals high in the tops of the trees. It was easy to find shelter and, anyway, Ashok reckoned the storm would quickly pass and we would be dry again soon after. He was right.

"It is like life, my friend," he said softly staring into the distance as we sheltered under the huge leaf of a banana tree.

"Storms come, you cannot avoid them completely, you can only shelter. But the trick is in the knowing that that is all it is – a storm. It will pass. All of life's storms simply pass. They may appear to go on forever when you are right in the eye of the storm but none ever do."

I waited, watching the huge pellets of rain splash ferociously into growing puddles on the jungle floor.

"Search for the shelter in the middle of life's storms – and that doesn't just mean running to people who will look after you, which is the natural reaction. But it also means looking for the strength inside. We all have the tools and the capabilities and the strength to ride out life's storms, it's just that some have to dig deeper and harder than others to find that core." He glanced at me. "Do you understand what I am saying?"

"I think I do," I replied hesitatingly. "But it's not always that easy, is it?"

"I never said it was easy," Ashok said simply. "What is easy about clearing your mind in meditation from all that chattering monkey talk, calming down and becoming still? It is one of the hardest things to do. But practise, day after day, night after night, and when you hit one of life's storms, you can retreat into that inner space. Find the calm, the tranquillity and the knowledge that this is merely a storm. It will pass. Life is eternal. And it is all working out, in any case, for your higher good."

"That's it – the answer to all of life's miseries is to meditate." I could hear the cynicism in my own voice.

Ashok looked at me, his eyes surprisingly full of mischief. "Life is as simple or as complicated as you want to make it," he answered smiling.

"Meditation certainly clears the way for deeper knowledge, better understanding and therefore a happier, more peaceful and purposeful life."

He appeared to be waiting for my reaction but I had no energy to argue.

"If you find that too difficult at the moment my friend though," he carried on slowly. "Why not try a few simple breathing exercises? You will notice that when you are agitated or angry or upset, your breathing becomes short and shallow... your breathing reflects your state of mind – no?"

I thought about his point and nodded.

"Therefore the trick is to control your breathing and therefore calm down your state of mind – see? Simple.

"If your mind becomes agitated, focus on your breathing, physically take deeper breaths, right into your belly and that will force your mind to be more peaceful. Having a peaceful mind creates a peaceful body creates a peaceful environment."

At that point, the rains stopped, the wind dropped, and the Sun burst through the clouds turning the leaves, the grass and everything around us into shining, glistening mirrors.

Ashok turned to me and winked.

CHAPTER TWELVE

We ploughed on through the jungle, myself ever hopeful that we might just stumble across a camp or the airfield, or even another human being. But I was now starting to properly worry.

I reckoned we were now around day 16.

The food we had brought to last us for 10 days was starting to wear very thin and my spirits were dropping.

I was thinking more and more of home and, for the first time, I was beginning to regret starting on this foolish adventure into the Amazonian jungle in search of a single, stupid flower.

Instead I began to focus on all the flowers we already had at Kew luxuriating in the huge green-house behind ancient glass. I remembered tending to each one lovingly as it began to bud, then coaxing out the petals with tlc, food and water. And I remembered the heightened joy as finally the flower sprung into being - feeling like a proud parent as I quietly observed the hordes of visitors admiring my floral offspring.

I began to think about the feel of the wind in my hair as I drove out of the capital and into the country heading up to Canterboonarry. The feeling of freedom and joy as the countryside sped past, the roads grew smaller and the traffic thinned. Huge old oaks and sycamores lined my path back home. Chirping birds greeted me on the doorstep – along with Hector, the caretaker's gorgeous golden Labrador.

And then, as always, I allowed my mind to drift to happier times in my luxurious apartment... times when me and Sash had been to see a movie then staggered back late at night and fallen onto the sofa together snuggling and making slow, sensuous love.

Times when I'd cooked for her and we'd sat on the small terrace outside the lounge under starry skies, and watched the boats chug by on the Thames.

Times when we'd laughed until we cried out filming away from home...

"Ashok – aren't you worried?"

"About what?"

"About never being able to get home, about not having enough to eat, about not being rescued, about never seeing your family again?"

There was a pause.

"What is the point of being worried?"

"Because... because... be..." I felt lost for words. What exactly was the point of being worried?

"We cannot change what is, my friend. We have done our best and are doing our best but rescue is now beyond our capabilities. Once again we must learn to let go and be assured that when the time is ready, rescue will come. Or not."

Wow. This man was cool.

"But you are not thinking of rescue," Ashok stopped and turned to face me. "You are thinking again of Sasha."

"How did you guess?"

Ashok didn't need to answer. He meditated every day, twice a day. Someone with that amount of spiritual dedication is able to fine tune all his senses – particularly intuition.

"I was wondering whether she'd even missed me," I whispered in answer to his question. "Whether she knows I've gone? Whether she even cares…"

"Lots of questions."

"Yes."

"Do they trouble you?"

I paused to think. Did they trouble me? They were never far from my conscious. She was never far from my thoughts at all. But did the thoughts trouble me? I supposed they did, really. They meant that I found it difficult to sleep at night, they kept me pre-occupied when I should be concentrating on other things. Was that troubling?

"A little," I answered.

"Do you want my advice, for what it's worth?"

"You know I have learnt to value that advice."

"Then two things."

I waited.

"The first thing is to see things as they are, not as how you would want them to be - for in that way lies only misery."

I bowed my head.

"It is as it is – you would be wise to remember those words. It is as it is…." He paused.

"You need to learn to live in the present and enjoy what is around you instead of grieving for the past or looking too far ahead and planning the future.

"Certainly plan for the future but write those plans in pencil. Don't be rigid. Don't be attached to your plans for that will only lead to disappointment. The universe has a bigger plan for you which may not fit into your own tiny ideal so be prepared to be flexible, laugh when things go wrong. Understand events happen for a reason. There is no such thing as coincidence."

I let his words sink in.

"And the second thing?"

"Learn to let go."

"That's not so easy."

"It takes practice but it is the only way towards a trouble-free mind. Towards peace. Towards nights spent sleeping instead of tossing and turning. Towards being in the present, in the now, properly alive, not day-dreaming towards an impossible future."

"Sometimes I swear you can read my mind."

"Letting go is the hardest thing in the world and yet the only way to truly live. If something is meant to be, if that is your destiny, it will happen. In the meantime all that you are doing is helping to make yourself ill by worrying. What is the point? It will not bring you any closer to her, it will merely harm yourself. Again, what is the point? Concentrate on other things close to your heart and if she is the one for you, she will come to you, you do not have to chase, you do not have to worry, it will happen. It will be your karma."

I thought about what he said. "Can you help me?"

"We can meditate, if you like? I believe you may now be ready."

It had been more than a million years since I had last meditated. My thoughts involuntarily took me right back to the time in the Ashram when it was mandatory night and day. It had been one of the reasons I had wanted to escape. I could see no point to simply sitting, cross-legged with my eyes closed. I wanted to be outside, running around, laughing, shouting, crying even – anything but in this state of... of... use-lessness.

"I'm not very good at meditation," I offered finally.

"What is there to be good at?" came the swift reply. "You are either willing to help yourself or you are not. It is your choice. We all have the choice to heal our own lives – or not. What is your choice, my friend?"

I paused – what had I to lose?

"I choose to live."

"I knew that. You know the posture?"

"I do but its been a long time Ashok and I'm not really sure I can do the lotus position any more – or even sit cross-legged"

"That is not a problem my friend, the important thing about meditation is that you are comfortable and your spine is straight so the energy has a clear channel up your spine. You can sit on a rock if you like or even lie down if you must but keep your spine straight and the focus on your breathing, do not make it more difficult for yourself."

I nodded, looked round for a suitable rock, spotted one and swiped away some lush green tendrils from a beautiful palm plant before plopping myself down. I closed my eyes, raised my chin and placed my hands on the inside of my thighs, index fingers touching thumbs in an Indian muhdra.

Ashok simply sat on the floor.

"What would you like to meditate on?"

"Escaping from the jungle?"

"No. That is too mental a statement. We shall use that as an affirmation. I believe we should meditate on the planets."

"The planets?"

"Yes. By meditating on the planets, we can keep track of the days. Already we have been in here 16 days so it must be Friday by now, therefore it's Vendredi – a day to meditate on Venus.

"By meditating on the planets, I hope that at the very least, I can also bring back your interest in Jyotish as the most important knowledge you will ever be taught in your whole life."

I felt suitable admonished.

"Ok," I grunted. "Venus."

"Close your eyes."

I obeyed.

"Now, concentrate on your breathing. Do yogic breaths, take the breath right into the stomach and feel the stomach wall expand. Now move the breath up into the chest and then the shoulders and... breathe out, down through the shoulder, chest and stomach. Whenever a thought enters your head, simply return your focus to your breathing. Ready?"

I nodded.

"Ok, here goes. Breathe in.... hold... breath out. In again... hold... and out. Breathe in.... hold... and out.... In.... hold.... And out... Again, in.... hold... and out. Remember every time you hear an outside noise or a thought pops into your head, simply re-focus on your breathing. In... hold... and out. In... again hold... and out... In....

The whole jungle seemed to fall quiet as I concentrated on my breathing. It sounds an easy thing to do but – as anyone who has tried it will vouch – it's a lot more difficult than you would dream.

My problem was - and always has been - blocking out those unwanted thoughts.

Time and again I get my mind clear and then something will pop into my head – usually something to do with Sash, or my car, or the house, or my pals, or the orchids – just something which will take my mind away from my breath and set it racing again full-pelt down a fizzing road.

Practice makes perfect of course, as it does with everything, but I was well out of practice and right now my mind wanted to be focused on Sasha – not breath.

"Now," said Ashok, breaking into my thoughts, "Let us bring our concentration up through the chakras, feel the energy flow up through your spine, opening each chakra until we reach the third eye."

With an almost superhuman effort I pulled myself back into the zone and surprisingly felt an old familiar warmth steadily work its way from the base of my spine, up the centre, warm the back of my neck, go into my head and onto that point between the eye-brows – the third eye.

"Feel your spiritual eye open," continued Ashok. "Now picture Venus, that huge planet turning slowly in the universe. Think of the qualities of Venus, of beauty, of love, of luxury and the finer things in life." His voice was quiet, soothing.

"Embrace the qualities, sink into the planet."

And then it happened – totally unexpectedly. I was there. I was seeing the planet, and then I was sinking into the planet, inhaling it, feeling its gooiness smothering me but I wasn't afraid, quite the reverse, I felt ecstatic. I could feel a smile spread across my face and my spine naturally straighten, each vertebrae clicking back into place. I felt as though I was swimming in ecstasy and I didn't want to stop.

The planet swirled in front of me, over me, went straight through me in a purple glob.

I felt my skin tingle, my heart become buoyant and my whole being free from shackles.

Then, slowly, the vision, the emotion, the lightheartedness began to slip away, recede and disappear.

"Om, shantie, shantie, shantie.... And when you're ready, slowly open your eyes."

Ashok's voice came as from a distance and No! I wasn't ready, I wanted to stay there, to keep swimming, to feel my body as light as a feather, not a care in the world – but, too late, the spell had been broken. Reluctantly I felt the state completely drain from my body, gravity once again pulled on my body, the planet disappeared and all the sounds of the jungle returned.

I opened my eyes.

"I wasn't ready," I looked accusingly at Ashok.

He simply smiled.

"That was a taster. Something for you to remember. You won't get it every time but you will remember and you will always search for it again. Welcome back to true meditation."

Jeez. This guy was clever.

"And now we've calmed you down, we need to build up your strength my friend. Did you say you were Scorpio rising?"

I nodded.

"Then your lagna lord is Mars. You need to strengthen your Mars. Did your father ever give you a Mantra?"

I nodded recalling the time he had asked me to step inside his study in Yorkshire and made me repeat strange

Hindu words for 36 times. Being 12 years old at the time, I obeyed him because I had to but I cannot say that I embraced the idea. Ashok must have seen the flicker of irritation on my face.

He said: "I can see that you have the knowledge but not the wisdom, my friend. Wisdom comes from having knowledge and personal experience. The time has come for you to put your knowledge to experience."

I waited.

"I suggest you remember the words that he told you and repeat them morning and night at sunrise and sundown. See if they make any difference in your world this time."

"What exactly are they supposed to do?"

Ashok turned away.

"Patience, my friend," he said softly. "Seek and you will find."

And with that – he walked a little way away and sat down in meditation pose under a massive bamboo tree.

I was getting a little tired of his riddles but at the same time I was hooked, and lets face it, there wasn't a great deal else to do in the jungle apart from walk or sit and wait to be rescued. It wasn't quite sunrise or sunset but, nonetheless, I decided to try and put his words to practise.

"Om man mangy aha…?" Was that it? No. "Um man ongolga namaha?" That sounded a bit better but I still wasn't sure.

"Ashok?"

"Yes?"

"Sorry to bother you."

No answer.

"But I was wondering if you could help me with the Mantra? I'm sure it went along the lines of 'man um mangol aha' or something."

There was a pause.

"Om Ung Mangalaya Namaha."

"That's it, that's it! Say it again."

"Om Ung Mangalaya Namaha."

I started to repeat the now familiar Mantra under my breath.

"Thirty six times," said Ashok then closed his eyes again.

Thirty six times... here goes....

CHAPTER THIRTEEN

I woke up the next day to find the hot, hot sun smiling over the whole of South America - or so it seemed - and certainly seeping into every single living thing that haunted the jungle floors and canopies, teasing them out of their holes and hives to strike up a cacophony of excitable chirping, chirupping, cawing and squawking.

The jungle was a damned noisy, smelly, hot, humid, eye-wateringly colourful but fabulous place and today it felt good to be alive – despite the horrific reality which was staring us in the face.

I had got up early and washed myself in the river just as dawn was starting to break. Now I was back at the clearing where we had made our camp for the night, had dressed and fished out a small biscuit to nibble on as I eyed Ashok who was packing our bags ready to leave again.

"I do feel a difference." I said to his back.

Ashok eyed me and nodded sagely. "The Mantra?"

I paused and weighed up the words. "Yes," I said slowly. "I'm not sure if it's the meditation, the Mantra or the jungle but I feel so much calmer than yesterday when, in fact, I should be getting more anxious."

Ashok's eyes swept the floor before he moved some long grass off a stone and sat down elegantly in the lotus position. "What you are doing," he said – also choosing his words carefully. "...Is extremely powerful."

I sat down too, aware that was he was about to say had great importance.

He smiled. "You are connecting with the universal consciousness – through Mantra, through meditation, you are raising your spirit to the highest level. At that level there is no pleasure or pain, there is only bliss and an ever-lasting knowledge and wisdom of time eternal."

He paused and the very wind in the trees appeared to still to listen to his words.

"The Mantra connects through sound vibration, the very sound that made the Universe – the Aum. Given by a guru and with the correct pronunciation and sentiment behind voicing the Mantra, you are connecting with the Supreme Power.

"The Meditation connects your soul with the Ultimate through making your mind still and becoming one with all of life. With stillness of mind you cannot be drawn into the dramas of life. You can see the drama for what it is – a learning tool – and you can choose your reaction in an intelligent, measured way. That is to say you will choose to stay calm amidst any drama in your life and understand what you can learn from that drama rather than be entangled in life and subject to intense emotion.

"Through the meditation then and the Mantra, you begin to release your karmic bondage from the causal body. You stop reacting to situations in the age-old way and re-educate yourself to be calm in all situations. Eventually you reach a state of equilibrium which leads to enlightenment and pure bliss.

"In this way, the vedic astrology that your father practised, that you were first subject to as a child, and that I have had the honour to learn, can help."

"In what way?" I asked, knowing the answer but wanting a verbal explanation.

Ashok paused. "By showing people the cause of their suffering – opening their eyes to the cosmic plan. A good astrologer – and by that I mean someone with an innate ability plus experience in this lifetime – can open your eyes to your very own dreams, can tear away the blindfold from your eyes and open you up to life's wonderful realities and opportunities. A good astrologer can show you your own life's purpose thus starting you on the path to self-realisation, faith, hope and the divine."

Ashok stopped and looked at me. "Does that make sense to you?"

"It does – and it doesn't," I answered, trying to taking it all in.

"There is duality in everything," he smiled affectionately and shut his eyes.

There was more silence as I reflected on his words and then was reminded of something I had meant to ask a few days ago.

"Ashok?"

"Yes, my friend."

"Remember a few days ago when you were talking about vedic astrology and asking about the planetary placements in my chart?"

Ashok nodded.

"Well... you seemed to suggest that I was about to embark on a huge adventure – what was all that about?"

Ashok furrowed his brow in concentration.

"If I remember rightly your Sun and Moon were in your 10th house of career which was Leo?"

"Yes," I concurred.

"The Sun is very strong as it is in its own sign and in Mooltrikona. The Sun is our soul, its where we shine and the Moon is our mind, our emotions, our psychological make-up so therefore you have a very strong house of career."

I shrugged. I guess it was right.

"The interesting thing is that you are currently in your Mars dasha, that is to say that you are in the dasha or timeframe ruled by your very own ruling planet, your Lagna Lord – Mars – which makes this a time for doing exactly what you want to do, for finding yourself and coming into your own."

I nodded again.

"But very soon you will change dashas into Rahu. Rahu is a node of the Moon which signifies excess. It is also about foreigners, maybe travelling abroad. Rahu is in your seventh house of relationships so you would naturally expect there to be many relationships during your Rahu period and maybe relationships with foreigners."

I raised an eyebrow.

"Not necessarily intimate relationships," Ashok smiled. "But many relationships of one sort or another – it could very well mean a step into the public domain."

I considered his words.

"I am probably already in the public domain through my television work," I offered.

"True," said Ashok, nodding. "So think what will happen when you enter the Rahu period which is all about excess..."

His words hung in the air.

"But how is that connected with an adventure?" I asked eventually.

"The seventh house is 10th from the 10th therefore it too, carries connections with your career. Your career is where you shine and Rahu is about excess in your house of relationships…"

I waited.

"I feel, my friend," Ashok said slowly turning to me. "That for some reason in the not too distant future, your profile will be raised well above that of ordinary TV gardener, well beyond the shores of the UK, and it is your destiny to understand that and decide how to react and how to handle that…"

"Ashok?"

"That is enough for now my friend." Ashok stood up swiftly to signal the end of the conversation. "We must carry on walking."

I waited until he passed me and then dropped into line behind as my mind went into overdrive.

Walk?

He must have been joking.

How on earth could I do anything other than skip, jump or bounce through the jungle when I'd just been told that my destiny was going to go well beyond the boundaries of Britain and that I was going to shine beyond my wildest dreams.

Alan chuffing Titchmarsh – move over! Big TIME!!

I was on my way.

I would find the biggest, most beautiful, succulent, gorgeous, orchid in the whole world and return home as a national hero. My reputation would spread worldwide and soon botanists from around the globe would be knocking down my door asking me to join them on an exploration of the Amazonian rainforests for the bunga bunga flower, or trip down the Nile in search of the woopa woopa berry or even climb the foothills in Papua New Guinea fervently looking for the chippa chippa starling petal.

The world would be my oyster. I would be filmed (naturally), have my own documentary show, be feted, a movie would be made of my entire life starring Brad Pitt and Angie whatsit…

And Sasha, of course, would be literally begging for me to take her back. She would dump her wimp of a husband, scoop up her twin boys and be on her knees asking for forgiveness and access into my sumptious boudoir.

Ahhhh…

Life would be so sweet…

"You are distracted my friend?"

It was Ashok, once again breaking into my multi-coloured day dreams.

I pretended not to hear him.

"Is it your ego?"

MAN. How irritating was this fella? You couldn't even enjoy some peaceful fantasising without him knowing what was whirling around in your grey cells.

"I suggest you may need to meditate." He said this without even turning round.

Immediately I felt ashamed. Ashok was right, of course. My ego was going bananas. It was all about me, me, me.

"I was thinking about being famous."

"I know."

"I mean really, really, REALLY famous."

There was silence.

"Yes, I know."

"Because I discovered this wonderful orchid, and everyone treated me as a star and wanted me – even Sasha."

Ashok stopped and turned to face me.

"That may well be your destiny."

I couldn't help myself. I smiled.

"However…"

I knew that was coming.

"It has been said many times before, my friend, but we live in a culture obsessed by celebrity and materialism.

"There is nothing wrong per se about being famous. It is what you then do with that fame that counts. In a nutshell you can use it or abuse it.

"You may well find that orchid and become an international superstar loved and sought after by millions who want you to help them with expeditions, hear your daredevil stories, be simply in your presence.

"But if that were to happen, how would you behave? Many people would simply lap up the glory, believe they were better than the rest and deserved special treatment. They would treat their fellow human beings with loathing and distaste, believing themselves to be 'chosen' in some way. They would blunder their way through life creating enemies and bad karma whichever way they turned and, believe me, they would die miserable and be re-born having to pay back all of that bad karma."

I reflected on his words and felt the smile on my lips dissolve.

"However, there is another way," Ashok continued softly.

"There is the way that sees every single human being as being equal but at different stages in their own development. There is a path which has empathy for each individual's stage of development which is neither judgemental nor patronising.

"There is a way which recognises that with great fame comes great responsibility and an absolute necessity to behave in a manner which will only bring kindness and light.

"That way is by connecting with the Universal Consciousness and realising that all of your talents, all of your 'luck', all of your abilities are but a channel from creation. They are not yours per se my friend, they do not belong to you. They are given to you to be used for the good of the whole of humanity.

By accepting this view, you can become humble – still be great, still be famous worldwide - but use your unique position to be good, do good and bring peace to this world not more envy and bitterness."

"I understand Ashok."

"You will understand Christian, more than most because of your Ashram upbringing. You will have soaked up much spiritual teaching and wisdom almost by osmosis. What you need to do is to carry on with your meditations to re-awaken those teachings, and those from your past lives because I feel that your destiny is much greater than simply being a sought-after botanist... although botany may be your catalyst."

I felt myself frown at his words.

"No, don't think," he admonished. "Just feel my words speak to your heart and intuitively feel what is right for you. Close your eyes, meditate on that feeling and the right path for you will come. Don't worry, my friend, as with all things and all people - whatever is yours is coming your way..."

Chapter Fourteen

That night was colder than the others and I dug deep in my rucksack to see if I could find any extra layers. Instead my fingers wrapped around some crinkling papers, and pulling them out I realised they were from my old diaries and letters which I'd stuffed in my bag before leaving Canterboonarry Hall, the night before we left for the Amazon. I lit a match and read:

Hello Sasha,

What can I say? You have changed my life completely. From being someone who thought the days of wild lovemaking were gone forever I can now say they have only just begun.

I have never wanted someone so much in my whole life. I think about you all the time and find I'm aroused just by hearing your voice. I've lost twenty years in the past three months, a quarter of a year which feels more like three years.

You have discovered a side of me which has remained undiscovered for the past 36 years. It has been known to me but to no other person. I can speak to you in a way which I have never spoken to anyone else - or ever will.

I have discovered words and thoughts which I have never dared to utter in the past for fear of causing offence, even now I can hear myself saying things which up until recently I would never ever have said to anyone. To my delight you enjoy hearing this from me, even finding it a great turn on!

I can't believe how I'm behaving at the moment. It's like a dream - I know you feel the same way - It's like watching someone else rather than being me. I can't understand how such a dramatic change has come over me in the time we have been together.

If I'm honest I wanted to make love to you from the moment I met you and often thought about this in the privacy and safety of my head. The reality of the relationship we have is far stronger and sexier than anything I could have imagined.

I love the way you dress to please me - because it pleases you too. Not just because it's what I like, but because its what you like too. I'm having the best sex ever and there have been a fair share of women in the past, but I've often called a halt before things really took off. I've never really wanted to in the past, never had the appetite - but with you I can't get enough. I just hope you don't get bored.

It's more than sex, but this is an essential part of our relationship. I'm showing you how much I love you by wanting you all the time. I've never felt like this before.

All this talk about sex though wouldn't mean a thing if there wasn't a spark between us. I wouldn't be able to perform at all if I didn't have any strong feelings for you and I wouldn't have gone this far if I didn't love you. I've never been one for just a physical relationship.

I know I annoy you at times and you do the same for me. This is unavoidable in a truly passionate relationship. I hope it continues for a very long time and with a bit of luck it will. I'm here for the long term and will always be there for you. Just put up with my strange moods from time to time. You are getting to know the real me, not the public version everyone else has. It must be a bit of a shock to your system to discover a person you were maybe not expecting - a more exciting and unpredictable version of what you thought you were going to get. A bit like yourself really.

Quite simply - I love you very much.

Christian

I crumpled up the letter and put it back into my ruck-sack, pushed the rucksack under my head and laid down, closed my eyes.

I had been feeling a lot better today from doing the meditation and the mantras but I still missed Sasha.

If I was truly honest with myself, I missed her laugh-ter, I missed her conversation, I missed her body, I missed her humour, I missed the long, silly telephone conversa-tions, the sneaky kisses, the arguments even and most of all I missed her smile.

The smile that would light up my day, month, year.

The smile that played on her lips no matter what I'd done, no matter what had happened, no matter how seri-ous the situation. She would always see the sunny side of life. Always have humour.

I wondered whether she thought of me at all or whether she was just plugged back into family life, doing the chores, acting as a taxi, washing, ironing, cleaning. She probably didn't have time to give me a second thought – and that made me immensely sad.

"Watch your thoughts me laddo," the words crept into my mind, it was almost as though Ashok had woken up and was speaking to me again. "You create your own reality. What you think dictates what you are, what you become and how you feel. You can choose those thoughts. You are master of your own mind. It does not master you. Be careful what you think…"

I opened my eyes and peered into the dark canopy of creaking trees above me as I remembered a conversation we'd had about three days ago.

"We are all magnets my friend," Ashok had advised. "We attract what we are. If we are miserable, depressed people then we attract other miserable, depressed people who tell us what a miserable, depressed world we live in. If we are happy, joyful people then the same rule applies. Which would you rather?"

I had felt myself smiling.

"The thing to remember is that we all have choices. Each man was placed on earth to enjoy its fruits but some do not even see the fruit, some gorge on the fruit but the more sensible men admire the fruit for its beauty and allow others to share that enjoyment.

"We all have choices," Ashok had continued. "You can choose to be who you are – happy or sad, joyful or miserable, an inspiration to others or a drain on society and your friends and family.

"Other people may impact on your life and drain you of your joy and your enthusiasm for a short time but, again, you can choose how you react to those other people. You cannot change them or their behaviour but you can choose how you interact with that person and what emotion they will make you feel.

"If a lover leaves you," Ashok had gazed intently into my eyes. "Then you can either choose to be miserable and dwell on your misery for a very long time making others around you miserable too. Or you can accept that this is how your life was meant to run, that you are liberated and that even better things are planned for you. You choose to smile through the pain, your friends marvel at your resilience, enjoy being around you and invite you out so you get to enjoy life again. It is as simple or as complicated as that."

Thinking about that conversation I reasoned that I can't choose to think about Sasha all the time and be miserable. How do I know what she's doing or what she's thinking? It could be that she too was miserable, missing me like crazy and wishing she'd begged me to stay. Perhaps she was even wishing that she had decided to leave that husband of hers and carve a life out together with me? Now, that thought brought a smile to my face.

Maybe I was deluding myself but did it really matter when I was stuck in a jungle and might never escape anyway?

I could either choose to think that Sasha was getting on with her life and perfectly happy – which made me miserable.

Or I could choose to think that she was missing me like mad and was trying to reach me to say she had made a big mistake and wanted to live with me after all – and that thought made me incredibly happy.

It doesn't take a genius to realise which was the better thought to focus on.

And they do say that you make your own reality so thinking positive was a double whammy – firstly I got to be happier, secondly it had all the potential to make my dreams come true.

I closed my eyes again and smiled.

My dreams tonight would be joyful.

CHAPTER FIFTEEN

Life is fascinating.... as I said earlier, one of the things that Ashok told me is the fact that we are all magnets. What we are, we attract. What we think, we become.

Last night, having made the conscious effort to be more optimistic and think more positively about Sasha, our situation and life in general, the impossible happened – we found it!

Half way through the morning, we had just sat down for a rest near a small stream when Ashok looked up and gasped.

"Over there," he pointed.

And there it was.

The Ghost Orchid.

Seemingly floating in mid-air with its roots blending into the tree, the orchid was luminously white with two long petals twisting slightly downward. There was no doubt this was the elusive flower - but it was huge. I mean ginormous! Normally the flower is roughly 3 to 4 cm wide and 7-9cm long but this beauty was about twice that size – an absolute stunner.

"Wow!" I breathed, totally in awe.

"Beautiful," acknowledged Ashok stating intently at the bloom.

We both got up and walked as close as we could to the fabulous specimen. I reached out and just managed to touch its petal marvelling at how thin, dry and paperlike it felt.

"Wow," I repeated, lost for words.

There was a long silence as we both admired this thing of fragile beauty for which we had searched for over two weeks in sweltering conditions.

It was Ashok who broke the silence.

"What are you going to do?"

I turned to look at him, my fingers still caressing the petal.

"What do you mean what will I do?"

Ashok nodded at the flower and then turned his head slowly to look at me. Under the cream bush-hat, I saw his eyes darken.

"What will you do with the flower?"

I paused, looked at the orchid, then back at Ashok, feeling myself frown.

"I don't understand Ashok, what do you mean? What are you getting at?"

He smiled and sat back down on the forest floor cross-legged.

"Our senses create desires and these desires demand to be fulfilled."

I waited, a warm gentle breeze stroked the beads of sweat on my forehead.

"Not fulfilling these desires is the main cause of our unhappiness."

I turned my attention back to the flower. Its head bobbed enticingly in the gentle forest breeze. Its white loveliness beckoned, begging me to pluck.

"A wise person understands the lesson of desires is to control them."

"You're talking in riddles again Ashok, in Ashram talk. What are you trying to tell me plain and simple – not to pick the flower? The one that we have travelled thousands of miles to capture? The one that we have spent thousands of pounds on to possess? The one that – incredibly – we may even have to die for?" I gazed at him, feeling my frown deepen and the frustration well up.

Ashok paused, a delicate brown hand wiped away the sweat from his own brow and then he studied me closely. A twig cracked under his weight.

"You have come all this way my friend and spent all this money to see this very flower which now waves its blossom directly in front of you."

"Yes," I said in exasperation.

"And now you have seen this flower. Are you happy?"

"Ecstatic!"

Ashok glanced towards the orchid, still dancing in the breeze.

"Then why would you want to destroy that happiness – and the very thing that gives you such joy?

"Ashok what are you talking about?" I felt anger rise in my belly and I crossed my arms in front of me.

Ashok paused, and looked back at me.

"By plucking the orchid, by possessing the flower, you will kill it."

Another pause.

"By killing the flower you will destroy your own happiness."

"No, no, no," I admonished. "I'll take it back to Kew, cross pollinate, rear it."

"And then what?"

"Ashok. What are you talking about? You're a gardener. You know what next. We'll be able to sell them perhaps, make a bit of money, a bit of a name for ourselves…"

"And then what…?"

"I'm sorry. I don't get it. What do you mean – and then what? And then what - what? I'll go searching for the next flower I suppose."

"Exactly."

"What do you mean 'exactly'?" By now I was feeling very frustrated. I slid the ruck-sack down off my shoulders, squatted down, opened the straps and began to rummage inside to find my knife and jar.

"You will never be completely happy because once you have found the object of desire and possessed it, you then desire the next thing, something bigger, better, sweeter. And the object you originally desired withers and dies – taking a little part of you with it."

I felt the cold sharp blade of the knife at my finger tips but something that he had said suddenly hit home and made me stop.

Ashok continued: "It is human nature - don't beat yourself up about it my friend."

I looked over at him. "No, but what you are saying is actually really important. It's what I have always done, chased dreams, got what I wanted and moved on to the next dream. Chased flowers, women, got what I wanted and moved on."

"But you are not happy."

"But I am now," I retorted stubbornly, sweeping aside a growing feeling of unease. "I have found the flower that I wanted."

"But you've already said that as soon as you get back to Kew, you will forget about this one and want to start hunting down an even more rare species."

"Yes."

Ashok turned back to look at the flower.

"How would you feel if I were to suggest that you left the orchid right where it was."

"How would I feel?" I stood up swiftly. "I would think you were mad. Of course we can't leave the flower. This was the whole purpose of our journey."

"Only this one small journey. What is the purpose of our life journey?"

"Ashok." I knew my voice sounded impatient and that embarrassed me slightly.

"The purpose of our life journey surely," he continued ignoring my irritation. "Is to reach enlightenment, to be in the perfect state of bliss, to be happy and to make others happy."

More words from the Ashram.

"One of the ways to move towards this end is to be able to gain control of our senses and desires. The incarnating soul must enjoy the senses and fulfil their desires but people must not allow their desires to get out of control and allow their senses to rule their life."

I felt my anger slipping away and found I was now listening intently.

"This, my friend, I fear is what has happened to you."

"I...I...I..."

"It happens to many of us, do not worry, you are not by any means, alone."

"You are obsessed by an orchid, you must have it so you risk everything for possession, and then move on.

You are obsessed by Sasha, you risk everything to posses her – and once you have her, what will happen?"

I stared down at the ground.

"We don't even need to answer that do we?"

I sat down on a small rock jutting out from the under-growth, feeling deflated.

"So, what is the answer then Ashok? What should I do? With the orchid? With Sasha? What is the answer?"

"What exactly is the question, my friend?"

I sighed. "Please don't talk in riddles."

"They are not riddles. You are looking for something to make you happy. You think it is Sasha and you think it is finding the orchid. Why don't you simply ask – what is the key to happiness?"

"But that's what I've been trying to find all my life. That is the question I have been asking all my life," I replied in exasperation.

"And it has been eluding you all this time because you weren't looking in the right places. You were look-ing first for escape from your environment – as we all do. Then you looked for material possession to buy you happiness – as we all do. And then you looked to another person to give you happiness – as we all do."

"Then where should I – and everyone else - have been looking?"

Ashok brought his hands together in the form of a prayer.

"You must look inside yourself my friend," he said softly.

"The answer you seek is with you all the time. Happi-ness is about creation, it's about detachment, it's about understanding and fulfilling your destiny, it is about connecting and flowing with the universal forces to fulfil your highest potential. It's not about looking externally for someone or something else to make you happy. You have all the ingredients inside to create your own happiness. And once you find that happiness within yourself, you can take that happiness out to serve others, create happiness, make others happy too. Be still, listen to your higher self, find your unique purpose in life and pursue it in order to help others. That is the way to happiness, peace, clarity and to love.

"We all know that the happiest people in life aren't necessarily those with the best paid, most glamorous jobs, houses, spouses or holidays. No. They can be the junior school teacher who gives herself every single day in every single way to help broaden the mind and hearts of the young.

"It can be the nurse patiently serving, helping and healing. It can be the volunteer in a charity shop, consciously putting in their time and energy to raise money and help others. It can be the woman walking the animals day in, day out, through rain and shine at the animal shelter, sharing her love and making other living things feel better.

"Happiness is an inner calm, a state of mind that reflects the state of nature. It does not push, pull, demand, force or manipulate. It is as it is and it comes from within."

I had listened intently to what Ashok had to say but he was making me more and more angry.

"Oh my goodness, that is so easy for you to say," I finally snapped.

Ashok paused and dropped his head. "Not so easy as you think, my friend. Very few of us are lucky enough to come into this world and not have to learn the lessons

life has to teach us without first experiencing the pain
before transformation..."

I waited.

"Many years ago," Ashok continued. "My mother
was in nursing home in Delhi. She was the light and soul
of my life," he glanced up at me... "You would have
liked her."

I smiled.

He bowed his head again and continued. "The fever
came without any warning and took her life away while I
was but a few feet away sleeping in an easy chair enjoying
beautiful dreams... Up until that time I thought that nothing ever changed. I naively believed that my life would
continue.. getting up every morning, greeting the new day,
visiting the hospital, seeing to mother, watching her smile,
discussing my oddities, going to work, returning to the
hospital, going home. It had been like this for years."

He stopped to watch a bright blue butterfly softly
alight on the soft velvet green of a wide bamboo leaf,
then flutter by.

"When she passed away, I cried for days, weeks,
months. Every day I carried an ache in my heart which
became a huge burden, my shoulders stooped, until one
day I was walking through the streets of New Delhi and
I came across this beggar in an orange robe sitting on the
stone steps outside a Ganesha temple.

"I will never forget the look he gave me. It was a look
of great pity and I remember thinking: *'why is this man
in beggars clothes looking at me with great pity? Me with
my big house, my beautiful wife and fantastic job. Why?
When he has nothing?'*

"But you see my friend, he understood that it was
I who had nothing. My soul was empty, it was dry.

Whereas though poor he was in material possession, his soul was brimming over with the richness of life, of love, of beauty and of wisdom.

"He stood up when I approached and then smiled at me. His words were simple but they touched my heart and they are offered to you today and for you to spread to everyone in this world today to understand.

"'*Don't rely my friend on material possessions to bring you happiness for they are transient, will soon break and disappear. Don't rely on another person to give you happiness my friend because they too will leave one way or another. The only thing you can rely on is yourself. Be happy in yourself and with yourself and the rest will come.*'

"The very next year I lost my highly-paid job as a lawyer, my first wife and my wonderful suburban home. I turned back to astrology as a source of income together with working on the market, meditated a lot on his words – gradually growing richer in spirit.

"I then met my beautiful wife, we came to England, had three children and I found this wonderful work at Kew. Some might say I was lucky.

"But it wasn't just simply luck. It was awareness – consciousness of being. We have to be aware to be able to make the necessary changes. But usually we have to face loss and be taught lessons before we are even able to come to any awareness of this life and its deeper meanings.

"Knowledge only becomes wisdom when you live through personal experiences – be aware of that and never judge any other being harshly...

"You, my friend..."

I had been staring at the ground all the while he had been talking but now lifted my head to meet his gaze.

"You have not been taught such a traumatic lesson but it is still a lesson nonetheless.

"You turned your back on the spiritual path to find happiness and joy in the material world.

"The universe taught you that possessions did not last. It taught you that relationships can be fickle and do not often provide lasting happiness and now we have reached the place where you have right in front of you the perfect thing which is in your grasp to take and make you happy – but will it?"

I stared at the flower and bowed my head.

"No," I answered slowly. "It will not. You are right Ashok. Of course you are right but if the happiness is inside of me, how do I find it? How do I know what is my true destiny, the destiny that will make me happy? How do I discover why I was put on this earth and become happy with myself?"

Ashok fell silent for a few minutes before he said:

"There are many ways my friend – through meditation and offering yourself up, through prayer and asking for guidance, through talking with like-minded people but you are very lucky because you have one of the best tools right at your fingertips."

I looked at him, puzzled.

"Jyotish," he said, smiling. "Vedic astrology. The eye of the Vedas. The light on life. Your chart will show you the past karma that you have brought into this life and it will cast light on your soul's purpose. It is then up to you – through meditation, prayer, faith and action - to follow that purpose, be true to yourself and find your joy and happiness through connection with the universe."

"Jyotish," I murmured.

I had spent half of my life running away from the Ashram, from astrology, from meditation and self-realisation, to look for happiness in the material world. The material world had shown me only sorrow, desire and emptiness.

It had taken me to getting lost in a Bolivian jungle with an Indian colleague to show me the true meaning of happiness, the true route to happiness – and the key was understanding the very thing I'd been running away from: myself.

"Don't worry, my friend," said Ashok, clearly reading my mind.

"You obviously needed to be taught the importance of all those things you learned in childhood. It wasn't enough simply to be given them on a plate. But coming on this adventure, you have learned how to let go. You have re-connected through meditation and mantra to the original source. You were given the knowledge but you have added personal experience to bring about wisdom. I feel that you have re-discovered yourself and therefore happiness is yours from within. And that, my friend, can never be taken away."

I felt a smile break on my lips.

Ashok beamed back at me. "Now shall we make a move?" He nodded at the path behind us and away from the orchid.

I took one last loving look at the flower and felt an overwhelming emotion that it was right that it should stay there, living, breathing. I was happy to leave it be. To let go.

"One last thing," I said packing up my rucksack and swinging it onto my back.

"What about Kew?"

"Kew will survive," replied Ashok. "Naturally they will be disappointed but not distraught. Someone else will pick up the glory this time."

"But not us."

"No, my friend, not us. Shall we go?"

"Yes Ashok," I grinned. "Let's go."

CHAPTER SIXTEEN

Walking away from that flower, I felt a lightness which I don't believe I had ever felt before. It was a real sense of doing the right thing but more than that even, it was a feeling of – happiness. Pure, unadulterated, joyful bliss.

For a brief second I wondered whether I had actually gone crazy – too much time in the jungle. Maybe I had caught jungle fever? Sunstroke? High blood pressure? Mental exhaustion even...?

But in my heart, I knew that not to be true. I was happy because I had nothing – at least nothing that counted in the material world. And yet I had everything. I finally understood and held the key to eternal happiness. And that felt amazing. I was finally prepared to fully let go, to surrender, just to BE.

Suddenly Ashok broke into my thoughts

"Have you ever heard of Jagadis Chandra Bose?"

Our feet crunched through the undergrowth as I shook my head.

"Jagadis was a great scientist whose work and inventions put India on the science map of the world," continued Ashok.

"In 1917, he opened the Bose Research Institute in Calcutta where scientists came from all over the world to train. Even now it is still a famous centre of research."

I silently wondered where his point was going.

"Jagadis is important because he believed that plants were alive and felt pain like any other living thing, but he didn't have any equipment to prove it so he invented his own instruments and did indeed prove that plants were living beings."

"That's a lovely story," I commented.

"It's not a story my friend, its fact. If you cut the branches of a tree, the tree screams. It's a fact. You should treat every living thing with the same respect for they are all borne of the same stardust. Hurting someone or something else, physically or verbally, only ends up in hurting yourself for it goes against the laws of nature, the laws of the universe. The universe wants harmony, peace and love. Abide by those rules, hurt no-one and nothing will hurt you back. Simple."

"Another reason why it would be wrong to take the flower."

"Yes," Ashok smiled. "Another reason."

CHAPTER SEVENTEEN

It wasn't long after we'd spotted the orchid, that the second miracle of the day happened.

From a great distance away, over and above the sounds of the forest, we heard the distinctive whirring of helicopter blades.

Ashok swiftly dived into his rucksack and deftly lit an emergency flare which seared through the forest canopy and exploded hundreds of feet above our heads.

Within minutes we heard the helicopter high above us and Ashok raced to a clearing in the forest, pulling me with him.

Seconds later we saw a rope ladder twisting its way down into the clearing and I felt my eyes well up with tears. At long, long, last we were safe.

"Don't worry my friend, you will be fine." Ashok grabbed hold of the rope and gestured me to climb.

"I know," I replied, taking the rope in one hand.

"I'm just slightly worried that I'm returning to everything that I had run away from."

"But you are not returning the same man. The jungle has changed you."

"You have changed me, Ashok. Your words of wisdom have struck a chord in my heart."

Ashok shook his head. "Any words that I have spoken have merely articulated what is in your heart already. Now quickly. Climb."

We both fell silent as we were winched up through the tree-tops and yanked from the sweltering jungle floor.

It was the pilot who gave us a sense of what was to come – although I was barely listening.

"Welcome aboard boys," he shouted above the noise of the blades. "Seems the whole world is awaiting your return."

CHAPTER EIGHTEEN

There were a million flashbulbs. No, I mean it. One million flashbulbs - without a word of a lie.

We touched down on the same airfield where we had landed what seemed like two years ago, and we were suddenly surrounded by a baying crowd: television cameras, lights, people shouting our names, pulling us this way and that. It was total, absolute mayhem.

"Here Christian."

"Over here."

"BBC News Christian, can we have a word please?"

"NBC, what was it like in the jungle?"

"Did you think you were going to die?" (This from a highly attractive blonde girl with a microphone, I smiled at her and she winked back!")

"Christian – what would you like to say to all your fans?"

"Ashok, how did you survive?"

A tall woman with reddish-brown hair appeared from nowhere and grabbed my arm dragging me away from the helicopter pad and towards a small ramshackle-looking building a few yards away.

"Five minutes gentlemen, then you can all have your interviews," she yelled above the mob.

I looked back to see what had happened to my friend and it was then that I saw HER.

She was standing behind everyone else at the far end of the helicopter pad and she was wearing a long cream mac, wrapped tightly around her slim body. Her long brown hair blew in the wind from the blades.

"Sasha," I whispered, barely trusting my eyes.

Wrenching myself free from the PR lady, I dived through the startled mob towards the woman of my dreams.

She was smiling and for a second I thought it might just be that – another of my fanciful dreams.

Racing up to her I stopped, panting heavily.

"Sasha? Is it really you?"

She nodded, a huge smile breaking out across her beautiful face.

"Hi Christian, what took you so long?"

There was no more need for any more words. I grabbed hold of her, swung her off the floor and completely snogged her face off to the sound of three thousand camera clicks. The press men whooped with delight.

CHAPTER NINETEEN

"What happened?"

"What do you mean, what happened?"

I looked deep into those beautiful chocolate brown eyes smiling up at me.

"You know what I mean…"

She shrugged and smiled again. The corners of her eyes crinkling seductively.

"I learned that I couldn't live without you."

"That's not true," I retorted laughing but feeling pleased nonetheless.

There was a pause.

"If that's not true… what is?"

I looked again into her eyes which had darkened momentarily. She walked away from me towards the window and gazed out across the tarmac of the small air strip to the edge of the green jungle.

We had escaped momentarily from the airfield and the world's press and holed up in the ramshackle hut where our jungle adventure had started seemingly eons ago.

"It's a cliché that you don't know what you have until it's gone," she said, still staring out of the window. "But I guess clichés are clichés because they have been said so many times - because they are true." At that, she turned to face me, her form silhouetted against the window.

"I missed you when I had to say good-bye. I didn't want to ever say those words...but I didn't like the way that our relationship made me feel. I didn't like having to lie to my husband," she hung her head. "And I didn't like the seediness of our meetings and the unreality that we had to share."

I stayed silent while she paused, seemingly hunting for the right words.

"After I said good-bye, I missed you so much. I threw myself into work to stop thinking about you night and day. I purposefully drove miles around London to avoid seeing places where we'd met, where we'd kissed, eaten, laughed..."

I put out a hand and gripped the back of a chair to stop my knees from buckling underneath. Sasha looked up at me, sighed and then turned again to look out of the window.

"When you rang that day..."

I felt my fingers grip harder.

"When you rang to tell me you were coming here... to Bolivia... I... I... I just fell to pieces. I tried to hold it together on the phone but I felt something inside me just die."

"Sasha..." I released the chair and strode over to her, sweeping her into my arms.

"No," she fought back to release my hold. "No, let me finish."

Reluctantly I dropped my arms and stood next to her at the window.

She swept a stray piece of hair out of her eyes and looked up, searching my eyes for I knew not what.

"It was at that moment Christian that I realised that I loved you. That I'd always loved you and that I had allowed you – no - *pushed* you even, out of my life. The best thing that had ever happened to me, I was pushing away."

"Then why didn't…"

Sasha held up her hand to silence me.

"I was paralysed. I wasn't functioning. My head was telling me one thing and my heart was screaming another so I made up my mind to wait. It would only be 10 days I told myself. Perhaps a little longer. But we had waited so long already, we could manage a few days more."

"And then what happened?" I prompted, scarcely daring to believe what was happening, what I was hearing. On the face of it I remained incredibly calm – you would have been so proud of me, dear reader - but inside, I could literally hear my heart thumping, my chest was swelling and it was all I could do not to simply grab her in both arms and whisk her straight off to a damned good hotel room and…and…well… orchid fever was gripping me, enough said….

"I spoke to Steve."

"Steve?"

"Yes, my husband."

"I know who Steve is…" I could feel my mouth literally dropping to the floor.

"I told him that I didn't think it was working. I told him I wanted to leave…"

"Leave..?" My God, I thought I was going to faint.

"I told him about you."

I reached out, grabbed her hand and held it tightly.

"Then after two weeks I called your boss."

"Mushroom Man?"

"Yes," she smiled.

"What did you say? Who did you say you were?" I whispered hoarsely thinking that any moment I was going to wake up from this wonderful dream.

Sasha coloured.

"I said I was your mother."

"Hah, wonderful!" I exclaimed, finally allowing myself to enjoy the moment, and trying to imagine the expression on Mushroom's face.

"I wanted to know when exactly you were due back. I think he'd actually forgotten you'd gone."

"Doesn't surprise me," I murmured.

"Anyway, he realised straight away that there was something amiss. Said he'd call me back and disappeared off for about an hour – I assume to make some phone calls."

I smiled and pulled up a wooden crate to sit down.

"When he eventually called me back, he sounded absolutely terrified. Said you were expected to be on a plane home four days previous but no-one from base camp had seen you for over two weeks. It was at that point that I, too, started to panic."

"That was probably just about when we realised that we were lost."

Sasha knelt down next to me, reached over and took my hand.

"I was terrified I would never see you again."

I smiled. "I felt exactly the same way."

We stared for a moment into each other's eyes silently acknowledging a force greater than the pair of us. Then she stood once more and leaned against the wooden window ledge.

"We waited for one more day to see if there was any news and it was the longest 24 hours of my life. I called back Mushroom Man, but this time, told him I was your producer and said I needed contact numbers. I then called my exec, told him the story, said there was a potential doco, could I be financed to go film in Bolivia. He rang News who also put a VJ on the case and three of us caught the next plane out of Heathrow."

"You're amazing," I breathed, gazing in open admiration.

Sasha smiled and warmed to her theme.

"When we got here, it was a case of hiring a chopper and then waiting. When nothing appeared to be happening I suggested to the news guy, Martin, that he break the story and he did. 'TV Gardener Searching For Priceless Exotic Orchid Goes Missing in Amazonian Jungle.'"

"That explains all the press."

"It went global Christian," Sasha said softly.

"Must have been a quiet news day," I grinned.

She smiled back.

"The story was picked up on all the wires and then, when we got the call that they thought they'd found you... well... everything went crazy... people were flying in from all over the world."

"Mad," I said, then stood up and kissed her, full, on the lips. An absolute knock-your-socks-off snog. Fantastic.

And I was just about to go in for the killer clinch when there was a knock at the door and it flew open to reveal a grinning Ashok whose face swiftly registered surprise when he realised what was happening.

"Oh, I am so sorry," he said, stepping back and pulling the door behind him.

"No, Ashok, wait," I dropped Sasha and bounded to the door, yanking it back open and feeling my face break into a massive smile. All was well with the world. In fact, it was better than just well, it was magnificent. "Come in, come in – come and meet Sasha," and I waved my hand triumphantly.

"Ahhh…. Sasha," Ashok looked over at Sasha and then back at me with an equally big grin on his face. He then walked over to Sasha holding out his hand. "I have heard a lot about you my dear over the past couple of weeks."

Sasha blushed prettily and lowered her eyes. I don't think I had ever witnessed her be embarrassed before.

"It's good to meet you," she said, shaking Ashok's hand.

Ashok turned back to me. "You let go my friend, and by letting go you released the energy, you allowed the universe to weave its magic in its own time without force or manipulation – and look what happens.

"What is on the outside is a reflection to what is on the inside. Your heart and mind are no longer in turmoil, you are connected again with the flow of the universe. Your mind is calm therefore your world is calm. You have learnt well my friend."

But I did feel slightly confused and felt myself frown.

"But is it right to have any kind of relationship at all if happiness comes from within and the main lesson is letting go?"

Ashok paused before fixing me with his gentle brown eyes. He said: "What you had before was an unhealthy, unequal relationship which wasn't free to express itself. You were dependent on someone else for your happiness which is wrong. It means you have lost your centre, your self-worth, your self-esteem and soul.

"You must find happiness within yourself before you are ready to join with someone else - not drain like a leech from another person or another thing.

"Love is a special gift which needs freedom and space to flourish – just like a flower, like an orchid.

"Of course, we humans are made to be in relationships and that is right and natural but they have to be healthy and balanced. Allow love space, allow love room to grow, allow it to beat in time with nature, then it can be the most beautiful thing."

He looked over at Sasha, smiled, then turned back to me. "Anyway, my friend, I was just coming over to see how you were. The PR lady wants us to do interviews to the press about what has happened."

"Ah."

Ashok's voice turned softer again. "I was just wondering what you were going to say."

I stared at him for some moments. "What would you have me say dear friend?"

There was a silence.

"I don't believe that I am the one to tell you anymore. I believe we should meditate and the answer will come."

I smiled gently at this wonderful Indian man who had been my companion for the last two and a half weeks, sustaining me through the most intense period of my life ever, and I nodded. "I agree."

I turned to Sasha.

"Sasha, we have such a lot of catching up to do and I honestly can't wait to sit down properly, to talk and be together."

She smiled.

"But I need to do this press conference and it could be the most important thing that I do in my life so I want to get it right – and to do that, I need to be on my own for a while, and silent."

Sasha looked at me long and hard, and for a second I cursed myself for perhaps making the wrong decision but then she spoke.

"I think you are quite right," she said, swiping away a stray hair from in front of her eyes. She bent down and picked her bag up from the floor, tossing it over her shoulder. "We have all the time left in the world to talk. I think you should have a really good think about what to say to those press men out there as it is liable to make or break you." She walked to the door, reached out and took the handle, then stopped and turned round. "Can I just give you one piece of advice?"

I waited.

"Speak from the heart Christian," her eyes bore into mine. "Don't allow your ego control, speak from the heart."

I nodded at her and smiled. "That is exactly what I intend to do."

She smiled back, opened the door, walked through and was gone. But this time I felt no fear, no gnawing tension, no sense of panic. This time everything felt just as it should be. This time everything felt right – because this time the time was right.

"Ok, my friend, do you want to be alone or shall we meditate together?"

I glanced over at Ashok.

"Actually, do you mind if I do this on my own?"

Chapter Twenty

So there I was finally alone.

Alone - but with the girl that I had always longed for finally by my side.

Alone - but with an amazing friend who had taken me on an incredible journey – not just through the Amazonian jungle but to the deepest, darkest corners of myself.

Alone - but never truly alone because I now felt the guiding hand, the Universal Consciousness, the Cosmic Creator, God – whatever name you want to use – more keenly than ever.

I knelt down on my own in that tiny room, next to the shuttered windows and words of wisdom uttered by Ashok through the cloaks of the night whispered in my mind..."*the way in which you embrace the present moment determines the way in which your future unfolds...*"

I closed my eyes, clasped my hands together and prayed:

"Thank you," I said.

"With all my heart I thank you. Thank you for delivering me safely home, thank you for teaching me how to let go, to surrender and accept what is, thank you for bringing love to find me, thank you for allowing Ashok to be a channel to share your wisdom and thank you for granting me this time to find myself, understand you and to learn so much about life."

I felt the flickers of a smile twitch the corners of my mouth.

"Now please give me the courage, the strength and the patience to fulfil my destiny, the one that was written in the stars so many moons ago. Help me to go out there and share the secret of happiness with others."

Opening my eyes, I straightened my back, grabbed the door handle, took a long, deep breath and walked out to greet the hordes of waiting world's press.

I knew exactly what I had to say...

THE END

Lightning Source UK Ltd.
Milton Keynes UK
UKOW04f1037100214

226188UK00001B/17/P